MW00953382

brief moments

ROBERT B. MCDIARMID

ROBERT B. MCDIARMID

Copyright © 2014 Robert B. McDiarmid

All rights reserved.

ISBN-13: 978-1497415553

ISBN-10: 1497415551

Cover Model: Doug Heacock
Cover Photographer: Brian Buckley

BRIEF MOMENTS is a series of once-a-day essays inspired by Julia Cameron's "Artist's Way" morning pages. They began as a daily writing exercise and soon became more than that. They became capsules, scenes, moments in fictional lives that readers began to resonate with.

The beauty of them for me is that the scenes come from so many different angles, places and perspectives. The viewpoints are not always my own, but an adventure in creating a believable snapshot - a moment, for the reader to consider. These daily briefs have reunited me with my creative spirit. This volume is arranged by the themes that organically showed themselves over a year of writing.

Briefs

More than few words....

FINDING COMPASSION

Our task must be to free ourselves by widening our circle of compassion to embrace all living creatures and the whole of nature and its beauty. - Albert Einstein

MISTAKES

Looking at him you could hear the Miles Davis that was jamming away in his mind, the soft curls of his hair seemingly moving to an unheard rhythm. The authoritative huff of the steamer at his barista station and the quick grind of the espresso seemed to be accompaniment.

"Triple spicy no-whip Mocha for….. Janet," he softly spoke, glancing up at the monitor to get her name right.

He reverently set down the large round cup, finishing the treetop design in the foam with a flourish. Janet walked up to the counter, stuffing a repeatedly laundered dollar bill into his tip jar. Not managing to look up from her smart phone, or even make eye contact, she collected her drink.

With a gentle smile, he turned back to his station and started the next order. Pushing up the sleeves on his t-shirt, he revealed a handwritten tattoo on his forearm. "Do not fear mistakes. There are none."

TIME STOP

The train station was full of morning commuters.
Conductors shouting all aboards for their train competed
with newspaper stand headlines and the angry woman
calling out names from the espresso shop. He always
waited to be one of the last off the northbound so he
wouldn't have to spend too much time in the zombified
queue into the station. Grabbing a morning paper, he
stood at the stoplight.

Across the intersection stood a man in his forties. He wore
a slight red beard, wire rim glasses, and an old-school
tweed jacket with the leather patches at the elbows. He
looked up from his phone and they caught each other's
glance.

The gentle happy smile that erupted across red beard's
face was infectious. The swoon happening between them
was palpable. It was that split second where a hundred
questions fired at the same time: What would he be like to
kiss? To wake-up to? Did he like dancing to old jazz? Did
he love coffee in bed with the New York Times on
everlasting Sunday mornings?

Pushing impatiently past him, not so gently pushing him
aside, a woman grunted, "The light is green. Asshole."

SALLY STRUTHERS LOVES JOGGERS

"I never see a happy jogger. I mean, you see cyclists laughing and talking. Guys at the gym smiling while lifting huge weights. Girls smiling their way through a complicated aerobics class, hell they even whoop and holler. But joggers? nope – the pained look of 'i am suffering'"

"That has never occurred to me, but man – you are right. the look of ultimate suffering."

"I think it's because they don't get rest stops with mochas, I mean, imagine getting a mocha then trying to run? No wonder the poor dears are unhappy."

"Isn't that why we cycle – so we can have as many mochas as we want."

"Of course!"

"Maybe we should start researching a way to get mochas to runners, we'd be like Sally Struthers but for emo jogger types. I can see the PSA...... "Do you know a runner?" you could play dramatic music in the background. "Steve runs 20 miles a day but look at him? He's miserable. Steve — is an emo jogger. Why is he sad? Because he can't have a mocha. He could have a mocha but it makes him projectile vomit just a few feet down the road. Help scientists figure out how to get runners a mocha for just five cents a day. Adopt a runner like Steve today – and make him smile."

"You are such a giver, so altruistic."

"I know."

MAGIC WORDS

The sunrise spread over the urban meadow as he walked quietly along, behind his cart. His brown clothes hung like Buddhist monks robes. This one had a drinking fountain, he could refill his bottles.

He had been teased by others in the underworld for living there. They called him designer homeless, the organic, free-trade vagabond. This was home. Their nicknames fell off him like water off a duck. He'd lived places where resources were scarce. Food bank passed out bags of rice. What good is microwave-for-ninety-seconds rice to an underworlder?

He laughed at the thought of some smug white city councilman suggesting installing a microwave in the tent city along the Guadalupe, or the center offering showers and "free access to a microwave." Processed food was bad for him anyway. Too much shit in that versus food. Fucking filler foods anyway. Fucking carbs.

He was distracting himself. Too much thinking. That was never a good idea. Keep on schedule, he thought to himself, keep on schedule.

Bottles filled, he made his way to the community garden where she greeted him. This one moment each morning reaffirmed him in a way nothing else could.

They'd met one morning, her catching him harvesting carrots from a neighboring garden. Her reaction wasn't shame or defense, but insisting on knowing his name. Nobody else cared to know it. She was Karen. Karen who loved her grandkids.

"Good morning, Albert" had become magic words.

HEAVY METAL

"Does it feel counterintuitive to be reading *Leaves of Grass* on an iPad with your earphones in listening to music?" he said as they were putting away their devices on the plane's descent.

"I don't think Whitman held a context in which to read his ideas. It's not a holy text or something, just poems from the 1800s. And even if I were reading a holy text, a Bible or a Koran, I think music helps me process written words better. I had a college roommate who got a 3.8 GPA in chemistry studying with Slayer pounding at 90db above the pain level."

"Slayer?"

"Heavy metal."

"Like iron or cobalt," he paused, giggling to himself. " See what I did there? Chemistry? Heavy metal? Cobalt?"

"Wow. And here I thought you'd wasted money on a college education."

"This is where the laughter happens, ya know, after a joke."

"If you have to go to that much work to explain it, clearly

it needs more work before it reaches laughter threshold."

"Or you simply don't appreciate good humor."

"When I see it, I'll recognize it."

IN 2048

"This article says that all fish will be gone from the ocean by 2048 thanks to climate change and pollution, " he said, looking up from his cell phone.

"I'll be 81 in 2048 and chasing orderly boys down the hall in my electric wheelchair in the all-gay nursing home. 'Come to daddy you little beauty. (bzzzzzzzzzzzz)'"

"Wow, seriously? I'm being serious here."

"Okay, sorry love. It's where all this has been headed for a while. I figure we will be eating entirely farmed/manufactured fish within 20 years. And genetically modified vegetables that will survive drought and other calamity. Our food system is in for a total change. If the harsh weather continues," he said continuing using finger quotes, " 'Science' will figure out a way to modify our food to survive. "

"Maybe we'll eat the primary food squares and octagons from Star Trek TOS!"

"But you mess with the food supply and those with resources to do so will hoard and those that are starving will starve even more. I shouldn't think about this stuff, it just depresses me."

The waiter arrived at the table. "Green Tea Smoothie? Chocolate Fudge Shake with extra whip?"

"How do you eat so many sweets and not look like a Macy's float?"

"Genetics darling, sorry."

"I hate you."

"Enjoy your Soylent Green."

STRINGS OF GRAY

We put away our suit jackets and put the ties back on the hanger in the closet. He came to me silently and retrieved the cufflinks from my shirt.

I went to the bar and poured a scotch, dropping a couple of ice cubes. I left it on the small side table next to his chair in the living room.

I went back to the bedroom, put on my favorite sweats and a ratty t-shirt. Returning to the living room, I found him laid back in his chair.

The strings of gray in his beard lit up in the sunlight striking his face from the window. I found myself stopped in my tracks.

"What are you looking at?" he said, dismissively.

"My beautiful husband."

"Oh good lord….. I may have been beautiful in 1993 but today I'm just a tired old mess."

I walked over to him and knelt between his legs and he held me in for a hug. He reached down and tousled my hair.

Holding me in tighter, he whispered, "I know today wasn't easy, lovey. It'll be okay."

TWENTY PERCENT

It's really very plain and simple; I am a coffee addict. Before you start worrying about that statement, it's not like I'm Nicholas Cage in Vegas, doomed-from-the-beginning kind of addicted.

Coffee addiction is different than crack. It is a metropolitan designer condition, because even in my most caffeine withdrawn state I would never resort to Folger's 'Crystals.' Even addicts have standards, darling.

The pleasure for me is a well-roasted cup of drip coffee that lingers on my taste buds for half an hour or more. That perfect balance of half and half, strong coffee and sweetener. It's why even on a 50 mile backpacking trip, a bag of Hawaiian Kona and a battery-operated grinder gets packed. It is the perfect companion to my morning sitting meditation. Twenty minutes of mindful silence compounded by fifteen minutes of coffee-sipping bliss. Truly it sets the stage for a positive step forward.

While I'm relatively sure the Buddha didn't drink Kona with half and half and two-and-a-half Splendas, he would embrace the twenty percent higher chance of me not killing anyone in the course of my day.

YOU SMELL REALLY GOOD

The leather bar was crowded. There must be some kind of event in town. He just wanted to be out and have a cold beer, smoke a cigar perhaps. He got his drink at the bar and found a good people-watching spot on the ledge a step above the rest of the patio.

He had already spotted a few lapdogs. The boys who cruise the crowd face to face, bulge to bulge so fast it looks like they are on an exercise program, like Midwestern housewife mall walkers.

He'd spotted the chosen: the men that held leather celebrity that people would fawn after and a group of men with them where status in the ranks was important. He'd spent his twenties in that group, polishing his leather, wearing sashes, producing events. Everything had its place in the world, but that wasn't for him now.

Now his leather was part of him and not a social status symbol. The leather he wore smelled of him, and rarely got polished by anything but sweat and spit.

These days he waited for the man that would walk by him, stopping a few feet away and glance back. He'd watch this man as he went back to a group of friends, occasionally looking up and catching glances. He'd look away for a few minutes and the man would find his way back to him. He'd introduce himself. They would stand closer than usual because the bar was crowded. The man would lean in and say, "This is going to sound ridiculous and weird, but the reason I came back to talk to you is that you smell really good." And he'd tell the man, a warm smile spreading across his face, that in fact, no, that it didn't sound weird at all.

ALL THINGS CONSIDERED

It occurred to him suddenly that he was over half way. That the years ahead of him no longer felt limitless. It wasn't difficult or hard to imagine himself at 60, 70, 80 or his 90s. But they were in reach, when it seemed that just a few years before he told himself, as much as you've done there is so much more spread out in front of you.

He knew that the next pivot point in his life was about to arrive. His sails would fill and push him off in a new direction. He felt surrounded by the right people, the right opportunities, and the right passions. Something incredible and powerful was coming, and would reveal itself as life had always done for him.

It wasn't fatalistic thinking. In fact, all things considered, coming up on fifty brought a wide smile to his face.

ASKING FOR HELP

"Some people ask for help but don't really want it."

"Why would you do that? Ask someone to do that and then ignore it, or worse, argue with you over it?"

"Well, sometimes people need validation, to hear "I'm awesome" and make the mistake of asking people that won't gloss over it. They don't ask 'take a look at this for me' seeking real criticism, they just want the creative equivalent of 'that'll do, pig'."

"But, he really is awesome, just not this particular project. And I'd be dishonest if I gave him a gold star for work I know is not ready for prime time."

"It's a lesson to learn, I guess, about how he processes criticism. It's a hard thing, ya know, opening yourself up to it. Hearing someone say 'that is not so awesome' or, let's drop the pretense, 'this is not your best work, and you can do a lot better' or worse 'oh this is terrible; you were really going forward with this?'"

"I would never say that."

"But perhaps your tone of voice does, or the fact that the feedback was provided via email, which has no tone of voice but the one the reader gives it. Perhaps he's a person that needs 'in- person' criticism versus e-criticism. Everyone processes it differently."

"Not all criticism comes from meanness. Some of it comes from people who genuinely desire to help you produce better work."

"But that might not be his experience."

DIFFERENCE

Uncomfortable silence fell between them.

"What does this mean?" he finally said.

"When I say I think I'm bisexual that is exactly what it means," his boyfriend replied.

"So…. do you want to act on this or…?"

"Well, we have an open relationship…and we've played with other people before…"

"Yeah, but all those others were guys."

"Does the gender make that much difference?"

He took a moment, thinking about it. "I suppose it doesn't… really…it is just new information to process."

"I will always be your husband. We will continue being respectful of what you and I have. The rules of engagement are still the same. You are my rock-solid relationship. It's just that my sexuality is a little more fluid and broad than I thought it was."

"But you know how we always give details afterwards, that might be a bit too much information," he said with a smile.

"Well, that is probably true. But…it is best that I bring it up, and we talk about it like we always have. So, we're good?"

"We're good."

"That being said, how about we go cuddle and watch some TV and then get really gay with one another before bed?"

"If we have to," he said with fake disappointment, "I guess I could fit some being gay into my busy schedule."

WEAPONIZED BARTOK

With an almost imperceptible click, the alarm clock began to spin up. The music flowed out in the room like the fingers of the perfect sunrise. He'd changed out the normal weaponized Bartok piano concerto for Copland's "Very Slowly" from *Appalachian Spring*. I smiled and laughed; when did he have time to do so without me seeing?

We'd been sitting next to each other on the packed commuter bus. I'd been listening to my iPod. I hadn't even noticed him. I'd been lost in the music, off to find my temp job doing accounting somewhere in the financial district.

The bus lurched to a stop, everyone in the sideways seats doing a simultaneous lean to the left like trees in the wind. He stood up from his seat. He wore the most beautiful long wool overcoat, and he had perfectly shined maroon leather shoes peeking out from underneath. Slowly moving up, I noted a perfectly starched white oxford and the most brilliant blue bowtie. That is when I realized he'd paused getting off the bus to look down at me, and missed the stop. He sat down and broke out a notepad.

"You are going to make me late," he said, looking up

through a shiny Cheshire smile.

The bus came to stop again, and this time he did rise to leave. He handed me a note and smiled again, saying, "Call me if you'd like."

The note was on the most delicate piece of notepad-sized stationery: *Pärt at 6:45 a.m.? That's a serious choice! We really should do dinner!* with his name and phone number embossed on the top of the note.

He arrived for dinner a few minutes early; I could spy him from my apartment window. His hair was slightly slicked back; he wore the overcoat still, but open to show a bright salmon t-shirt that fit him perfectly, and brand new blue Wranglers. He held a single white rose in his hand.

My phone suddenly buzzed to life in my hand, he was texting me, "You won't be needing that, so why don't you leave it behind?"

I greeted him at the door. We shared a polite but intimate kiss, and after putting the rose in some water, we were off to dinner. He saw my lifeless cell phone on the counter, tapped his off and setting it on top of mine, suggesting he'd come back for it later.

It all felt so natural. Holding hands on the way to the restaurant. Walking, although the tube would have been faster. Him so ever politely asking to get a real kiss out of me before going in the restaurant, in case he made an ass of himself before dessert and he'd never see me again. Laughing over drinks, enjoying bites of each other's dinner and sharing a dessert.

He came up to get his cell phone and didn't leave till the next morning.

He snickered, wondering out loud if having his own toothbrush on the first date was rushing things a little. Good lord was he great in bed. And we all know how we sleep after someone literally knocks our socks off. He'd woken about 4 a.m. and said he needed to get home, for me to sleep in, and that he'd see me again. He leaned suddenly while he was dressing and running his beard up my chest into my neck, he sniffed loudly and deliberately.

"You are so damn adorable," I said softly, half asleep.

"Oh, Mr. Robert, You have no idea."

You could almost hear him smiling as he spoke, "I have not yet begun to flirt."

It felt oddly comfortable to just let him dress in the dark, talking to me softly, then disappear like a ghost.

LITTLE STORMS

My husband has what I call, 'little storms' sometimes. He gets so amazingly angry at the smallest of things. I had never met his parents, and his siblings only briefly. I wondered what kind of origin breeds anger as the first response to any obstacle.

My stock? My father was a soft-spoken Presbyterian minister, and my mom, a quiet, reserved, humble minister's wife. Our home was books and it was often quiet as a library. Disagreements were cordial, but still defended, always with strength of the argument, never the volume in which it was presented.

Every once in a while, a fellow introvert will ask politely why I stay. Why live with such a volatile tempest of a man?

He always understands if I retreat to my library and read if he's playing music too loud or having an animated conversation with his sister.

But his little storms, are never mean, just angry. Some of them, like the one over the lack of selection in the gelato section at the local store, are fascinating, actually. We're getting this pouty over gelato selection? I have learned to respond with calm, without judgment, and give him some space until he starts to soften back up.

He's the only man I've ever known whom when he says 'I love you' I know that he absolutely means it. That makes living with any multitude of sins quite doable.

ONE DAY

The midwinter sun filtered through the redwoods, as he walked alone in the grove. His vest adorned with pins and badges that showed a history few could understand. This seemed to him like the place to be when the inoculations began up at Kaiser.

The *Chronicle* that morning had the banner: "A WORLD WITHOUT AIDS: THE END OF HIV." The world's philanthropists had come forward at a press conference to announce that not only had a cure been found, but that they would all finance its distribution. No one would have to pay for the vaccine.

He walked through the memorial grove at a time when most people were celebrating in the Castro. He walked down the stone steps into the back circle. "Walker within in this circle pause although they all died of one cause, remember how their lives were dense, with fine complicated difference." He slid over the edge and walked down the dry creek bed into the grove. Almost imperceptibly under his breath, he repeated, "thank you.. thank you.. thank you.. thank you."

A SHITLOAD OF PURPLE

She was an aborigine storm trooper. Everything matched. Purple UggBoots, purple stretch pants, purple skirt, purple jacket with purple fur on the collar. It was like she'd harvested the McDonalds character Grimace and wore it proudly like a woman might wear a fur to the opera. The sparkle lavender eye shadow finished the look along with shiny, long, weapons-grade purple nails. She stood as the bus slowed to a stop, and picking up her purple lame handbag, exited the bus.

"That was a shitload of purple," said the woman next to me on the bus, unsolicited. "It is obviously her signature look; a lot of work went into it."

"Do you think it started with the UggBoots in purple? Or the 'fur'?" chimed in another passenger, using hand air quotes around fur.

"I am stuck on what office environment that outfit is appropriate for," volunteered someone else.

"Well, she seemed happy and confidant, and that's more than most of us can claim at 6:45 a.m.," I said. "So her bliss is purple? Who are we to get in her way."

"That is such a hippy San Francisco thing to say," said the

woman next to me.

"Proudly so, actually. Doesn't make it any less true."

HEATHER

My sister is a beautiful woman. Honestly, she's funny, caring, exciting. But the bravest thing about her is what a fantastic mother she is. She understood, like our own parents did, that it doesn't always make you super popular with your kids. Teenagers and young adults are genetically designed to test boundaries, figuring out where they belong by testing the authority around them, particularly their parents. But what I've watched over the years is how fiercely she worked to make sure her kids had all the opportunities she had and a few unique ones along the way. She even took three girls from her husband's first marriage and figured out ways to make them feel safe and give them the ability to find their way even in the path of divorce, and the weight that places on children of any age.

She was there as each of them would discover something new, and smile back at her like "look what I just learned to do; isn't that cool?" And even when perhaps the thought of what they were learning worried her, my sister would smile back "absolutely, that's cool." I never imagined myself having kids. I mean, let's face it, for me having a schnauzer terrier is so much responsibility, I can't imagine having children. She has five beautiful daughters ranging in age from 17 to 25. She left her career to take care of her family, and as her youngest graduates high school next June, she'll be reclaiming parts of herself and watch more of her kids get married and find their own path. I'm sure she'll be just as fantastic in the role of grandmother as she's always been as a mom. Her relationships with her kids will change, as all relationships do.

At 47, I'm closer to my Mom than I can ever remember being. She still teaches me lessons every day, but in new ways. I'm absolutely confident my sister will find amazing ways to do that for her kids and grandchildren as well. I'm very excited to be around to watch it all unfold.

WE ARE ALL BORN SEXUAL CREATURES

"I can't believe you're still having sex, let alone with your partner," he said matter-of-factly.

I was so stunned by the sudden change of topic, that I was rendered speechless. And let's face it, rendering me speechless is really difficult.

"I mean, it's bad enough you tested positive," he adamantly continued, "but to continue having sex with people, particularly negative people? That doesn't seem reckless and selfish to you?"

A vicious part of me said on the inside, "Well, you'll never have to worry about having sex with me dear because I wouldn't fuck you now if you were the last man on Earth. You seem to be doing a pretty good job of fucking yourself with your faith anyways; I hope that works for you." But I think my actual response was something like, "I think we're going to have to agree to disagree on this topic. In future, you might keep thoughts like that to yourself, and I think I am going to go now."

I can remember this conversation down to every detail. I remember how it played over and over in my head for weeks afterwards. I was simultaneously shocked that a gay man would shame another gay man so nonchalantly, as if to suggest that "well of course, if you test positive, you should stop having sex of any kind with other people." First, there was anger that he felt it appropriate, across the sorting table at a thrift shop, to just blurt that shame avalanche at me. Second, was sadness for him, that he believed what he said to be true.

For a long time part of me said, "this is rural Idaho, and religion is deeply embedded here. Catholicism is particularly, powerfully shame-based, so be compassionate to his restricted world view." It's very sad that people wear so much shame on their heart for being gay. That even after they come out they continue to allow shame and guilt to shape and mold the world around them.

Although, I'd been positive for seven years, his question brought me right back to the beginning. I mean, it's no secret how you can get HIV. When I'd realized I was gay, and the kinds of sex I could then explore, I was really enthusiastic about exploring it. It wasn't like I ignored the threat of HIV. Finally being able to express myself sexually, after years of disastrous heterosexual attempts, it was powerfully liberating to learn how to make a man moan involuntarily. I was home walking the halls of the bathhouses, reveling in the sounds of fucking, watching men get completely taken away with pleasure. Once I learned where my talents lay, I set out to learn ways to make love, learn what parts of a man would send me to that euphoric place that only the smell of men can make happen.

That a disease is transmitted in such a deeply personal, and for some, spiritual way, it's a terrible thing. That a disease could make sex an ugly specter to be avoided, that someone could try and shame someone into letting go of that side of themselves once they have that disease, still makes no sense to me.

Marilyn Monroe is quoted as saying, "We are all born sexual creatures, thank God, but it's a pity so many people despise and crush this natural gift." Sex is one of the few things I'm not even remotely ashamed of. It's a powerfully unique way to communicate with someone. Whether that's catching a whiff of them while walking by in the gym, or up against the wall in a bathhouse whimpering, gasping and grunting.

BIRTHDAY PARTY

He hated party stores. Full of so much ill-manufactured happiness and joy that just the thought of being in one made him break out in a sweat. He liked his quiet life, his books, his cat. But she'd asked, and she'd get what she wanted.

He'd rented the helium tank and was inflating balloons in the garage at 2 a.m. Red, blue, green, yellow, pink, white. He carefully tied each with a slice of red ribbon, then onto a white string. He'd spent so many days here in his workshop perfecting it. Yellow siding had been easy, but the perfect blushy pink siding had been a miraculous late night spill of his pinot noir on the white siding. He remembered trying to wipe it away with a sponge and "blushy pink" had been found. He loved when parts of his work did that for him, just… revealed themselves. His work continued until there was a knock at the door. He looked through the glass and was surprised to see his sister standing there.

He had been there all morning, working. She waved through the glass.

"I just couldn't wait," she giggle-spoke like she had when she was "libble sisber" so many years before. "I just couldn't; can I see it?"

He wordlessly ushered her in and she saw it. There in miniature was the house from the Pixar film, *Up*, and he had been adding the balloons to it.

"Oh Larry, it's perfect. Oh gosh," she said, peering down and staring into the windows at the meticulously designed miniature house.

He stepped around her, unclasped the latch and gently pushed it open, revealing the inside. He'd found every detail. She imagined him sitting in front of the television taking snaps of every angle, every time he found a new detail writing it in his notebook.

"It is good work. Some of my most polished, I think," his voice tweaked really high from helium.

She turned to him suddenly, big reflective tears in her eyes.

"What?" he said in another high-pitched, helium chirpy voice, putting his hands on his hips.

They erupted in childhood laughter, as enthusiastically as his niece's birthday party in a few minutes time.

NICE

Typical bass thumping late night at the bar and that's when I notice the two of them in the corner. Here in the middle of testosterone alley, near a dance floor of grinding gays listening to the latest BritBrit remix, are two young college-age girls. They are clearly not having a good time.

In the fog machine humidity of the bar, I go over and introduce myself. Just speaking to them makes their eyes light up. They are Jen and Micha, both communications majors at State.

"So, why are you two here in the Garage on a Saturday night? Clearly you understand this is a gay bar, right?"

"Well, we were hoping we could make some gay friends. We're in San Francisco right? We thought it would be good for us to, ya know, be someone's fag hag."

My initial reaction was "oh my gosh, these young girls are cute," mixed with "what-the-fuck?" They think they're being progressive by befriending a gay man, but they're actually being completely offensive. Can you imagine someone going up to a black person and being like, "You're black?! Ugh, I really need a black friend. Can we play basketball and eat soul food together?"

Let me preface this with saying that the relationship between a gay man and a straight woman is a truly magical and special dynamic. The relationships I have with my girlfriends are incredibly rich, nuanced and incomparable to anything else. That's why when this beautiful young girl refers to herself as a potential fag hag. I want to shake her and say, "You are not a hag! You are a powerful goddess who gets laid way more than I do. Don't ever use that term again!" But, restraint is the better part of valor.

"This probably isn't the way, ladies. You see, the Garage is the gay man's hunting ground. And by gay, I mean buttsex and beards and cock. So, this isn't the place where someone is going to say 'Look at that pretty girl in the corner there,' like something out of *West Side Story*. This is just not the place for you."

"Here," I said, grabbing a napkin and scribbling some websites,"are a few local service organizations that are always hungry for volunteers. The way to meet a real gay man, and perhaps meet some part of the real San Francisco, gay men or bisexual women or transgender boys, is by organically going out in the community and doing stuff. They, I mean we, are everywhere, darlings. But, coming into our testosterone moshpit is not the way. Totes?"

They took the napkin and quietly left the bar. The

bartender scooted over to me. "What did you say to them that finally got them on the clue bus?"

"I was nice to them," I said, dropping a couple of dollars on the bar in tips, leaving and finding my way home through the foggy city.

WEDDING DAY

He had promised her he'd come. So he would just grin and bare it. His suit for the ceremony was in the plastic hanger bag behind him.

On the counter in front of him she'd left out a razor, shaving cream and some aftershave. "Good try," he chuckled to himself, as he pulled his long beard together in a tight braid. He actually did shave around the edges, so he could claim some effort. Without thinking, he splashed his face with a little aftershave. Oh good lord, it was Old Spice. Shit. There was no washing it off.

He arrived at the church in his construction man's pickup. It was the kind of whirling dervish that made people pray for his safety every time he got into it. Stepping out in the perfectly tailored dark green suit with a fresh flower in the lapel, even he had to admit he looked pretty good.

There she was on the stoop. She greeted him with a smile and a strong hug. "You smell like grandpa," she teased quietly in his ear. "Yes," he whispered back, "and revenge will be mine! Let's get your daughter married, now shall we?"

He stood in the center as the groom nervously watched

him and the back door of the church. He wondered what generational stories the boy had been told about the esoteric druid uncle from the woods. He winked at the boy, which didn't exactly have the calming effect that was intended.

His niece arrived in the back door, wearing his Mother's wedding dress. She strolled forward with quiet confidence. Beginning his opening words, he found his cadence and cast his spell over the crowd.

WORDS

I could feel him whisper on my neck, his beard close, and the impact of his words on my flesh from his breath bringing goose bumps. He was taller than me, and we learned on an early night out together how he seemed to fit in against my ear and neck. He always smelled of linseed oil. His lower torso sometimes pressing in against me like we were in a perpetual slow dance.

He never spoke out loud but breathed the words on my neck as we stopped to examine each piece. I was worried that we'd get in trouble with museum security for being so publicly affectionate. He repeated the words. We moved past paintings and sculptures, the space between my mind worked on his question.

Moving between galleries there was a reflective glass. We stopped a moment and looked at the two of us together. Looking into the reflection with me, he reached around me and caught my attention with his hands. As he repeated the soundless question against my neck, a Cheshire smile spreading across his face, then spoke to me in sign.

"What do you feel?"

OR LACK THEREOF

The train screeched to a halt between stations in the tunnel. Everyone let out a gasp of "not again" and retreated to their earphones and devices. All except two young twenty-somethings laughing in a twosome seat in the middle of the train. The sudden silence of the stopped Muni train seemed to amplify their conversation.

"I'm not a faggot or a meth head, so I don't need to worry about the AIDS," one of them giggled.

"Yeah, and now all the big guys at the gym are just that way because they get testosterone shots from their doctors because they're poz. Shit, perhaps that's what I need for my workouts to get better, some AIDS," the other said, both of them exploding in laughter.

"I'd just need to fuck some…" one of them continued, when a deep voice boomed in from behind them and said, "I think that is enough."

They turned laughing, suddenly not laughing, into the face of a policeman, as well as an entirely silent train of stern-faced commuters all staring them down.

MADAME DEFARGE

His entire outfit was a dark and murky gray, the kind that makes people worry that his iPod was loaded with nothing but boiling lava, Alanis Morissette fuck you anthems. He was always kind of scary quiet, the kind that makes you uncomfortable, like perhaps he was a modern-day version of Madame Defarge.

He sat in the corner of the coffee shop nursing a quad Americano. His hair was producted into submission. Everything about him was meticulous. He was watching me and another customer in line for our morning fix.

She made a large, overly complicated order: one with soy, one without, one third of a Stevia packet, one with Splenda, and both with just a 'puff of foam.' It was the kind of coffee order that was no longer about the coffee but a precision chemistry experiment.

"Fuckity fuck, I left my purse at home! Oh no!"

"Pay it forward, darlin',", I said to her, then, "Put it all on my tab, Vern."

The grommet-eared, flannel-clad barista behind the counter gave one of those "gotcha pal" nods and got to work.

She got her tray of complicated lattes and I ordered my simple French roast with room. I told my "joke" about half and half being almost as important as coffee for the thousandth time. Nobody laughed this time, either. The barista poured me a thick cup of joe and I moved to the condiments to add my cream and sugar.

I stirred my coffee. I always got coffee 'for here,' always wanting to savor the moment. It's how I'd first started noticing Mr. Gray in the shop in the mornings.

"That kind of kindness without hesitation is refreshing," said Mr. Gray, "Thanks for getting her coffee. Karma is rich."

It was revelatory what a smile did to the entire persona I'd created for him. His face lit up, shattering all my preconceptions in an instant. His eyes sparkled and his effusive body language changed him forever. He oozed a calm charm and wit I hadn't expected.

"Join me, won't you?"

SHOSTAKOVICH

He got up out of the water and stepped out of the pool. It was the kind of tattoo meant to be admired and seen in a pool where swimsuits were optional.

All etched in the darkest black and shadowed the entire length across his body were the treble and bass lines of a piano score. It was so intensely dark it almost looked like it had been bruised onto his flesh versus being drawn. The tattoo began on the back of his shaved head, down his neck, following his spine, through the curve of his butt and then curling between his legs and ending in a circular wave around and down his right leg.

It was actually thrilling to watch as he moved. I had, in comparison, an extremely small tattoo on my chest that I'd agonized my way through. I winced a fair amount thinking about how some sections of that must have hurt and itched after being done and healing.

He was equally beautiful and tattooed on the front of his torso, the specifics of the ink were obscured by thick black chest and stomach hair. Brooding eyes and a long dark brown goatee tied in an ornamental braid.

Across from me in the showers, he caught me at a full

stop, admiring him.

"Shostakovich…*Preludes and Fugues for Piano in E Minor*…is an intriguing choice for a body-length tattoo," I stammered out, revealing having stared at it long enough to recognize the score.

He didn't reply with anything but with a gentle, rich smile and a nod. I awkwardly excused myself.

Flustered, I returned to my locker to finish changing. I was getting ready to head home, when he was suddenly towering over me shirtless, wearing a pair of incompletely buttoned blue jeans. The smile still on his face, he looked down at me softly, acknowledging with another nod my tremble and I involuntarily swooned as I turned to look up at him.

"Sergei," he said, in a syrupy-think Russian accent, extending his hand for a handshake.

HAPPY NEW YEAR

He lit the blue candles in the windowsill before returning to his study. There, the blue candles sparkled at the foot of the Buddha, the driftwood he'd kept with him since childhood, the photograph of spirit house garden and other sacred objects in his private space. He lit a stick of incense. He stepped out of his robe and knelt in the darkness.

"I create sacred space in time that is not time," he began, "a place not a place; today is a day that is not a day; all malice and worry, now away, so all within here is right and just; this is a place of compassion, love, and trust. I light these blue candles in remembrance of those who are no longer with us and in thankfulness for continued health and fellowship. All these things I will bring others in the new year – compassion, love, lust, community, commitment, all these start with me and move outward like a ripple across a pond. I create sacred space in time that is not time."

He closed his eyes into meditation as the grandfather clock in the foyer rang twelve.

THIS MEANT SOMETHING

The dog walked up the bed, circled a moment, then collapsed in a gut bomb of a body slam. The wind blew outside with a horror movie howl. He put his arm around the dog, pulling the covers up over her. He could never sleep through weather like this; he just laid in the dark and listened. Pop had built the cabin strong, so he knew he was in a safe place. He knew there would be tree branches down everywhere, and chainsaw duty in the morning. The loft bed was the last place to get toasty, so he'd put extra logs on the fire before coming to bed.

He'd been to visit the ex and the kids the night before for Christmas. He'd passed out carefully thought-out gifts to his girls and even a polite gift to his ex, who didn't understand all the change he'd brought on them the months prior. He knew that inviting someone in like this, and risking a bit, was what the divorce and the difficulties had to be about.

Tomorrow he would arrive. They'd had a couple of fun coffee dates, and an extremely hot movie date on the couch at his apartment in the city. This was the first time he'd invited someone for the night. Seemed silly for a forty-year-old man to be so nervous and worried. He imagined that nervous dance of undressing and coming up here the next night. How they'd both smell of pine forests and sweat. He hadn't invited someone up to the cabin in so long, he wondered what it would be like. He chuckled to himself, knowing the dog would be upset; there would be less bed for him to have. But he knew they'd spend the night finding every part of one another. He imagined them smelling like each other by morning coffee, and staying that way for a day or so.

It was one thing to go on a coffee date with someone, another thing entirely to invite them here, in this special place. This meant something to him.

OVERSLEEPING

He rolled over in bed, stretching, when his eyes came level with the alarm clock. 8 a.m. and the train was at 8:42. Fuck. Fuck. Fuck. How did he do this? He raced out of bed nearly tumbling out onto the floor. Cursing under his breath, he stripped off his pajamas while stepping into the shower. He endured a lukewarm quick shower. He brushed his teeth, and combed out his hair and beard. He ran to the closet, and grabbed the nearest shirt; he had jeans on and an unbuttoned shirt when he reached the kitchen. He poured a quick cup of coffee, at least SOMETHING had gone right that morning. He buttoned up his shirt and grabbed the remote, flipping on the small television on the counter. He reached for the toaster when the emcee on the television behind him said, "Welcome back to Sunday Morning, here are the headlines…" He stopped cold as he heard a familiar snicker from behind.

His husband stood in the doorway, still in his pajamas.

"I honestly would have stopped you, but you were so determined, and so adorable, I just couldn't bring myself to do it!"

...RIGHT OUT OF MY HAIR

He sat in the shower. He almost felt guilty about wasting so much water. The scotch had tasted so good the night before, but now it had caught up to him. He soaped up the loofa and, to get his brain to focus, spoke out loud to each of his body parts, "Good morning toes; let's get you nice and clean." He figured a positive attitude, even a fake one, might get his mind out of the fog. He washed himself up and shampooed while humming songs from *South Pacific*.

It had been his first night out at a holiday party. It felt good to be seen. His friends had been careful to make sure the ex would not be there. They were watching out for him. He'd had all these wonderful plans, until his husband announced he was leaving him for another man he'd met "accidentally." He'd tried to be Mr. Nice Gay about it, and not be a pissy bitch. But being suddenly single for the holidays was beating himself up a bit more than he'd expected. The invitation to the party had felt like such a good thing. He didn't want to be one of those bitter queens wearing a veil and catting off about that bitch of an ex of his. No, tragedy wasn't a good color for him. Right now, he was just trying to move without feeling it at 400%. Feelings were the least of his worries, and that was actually pretty okay with him, considering.

HEALTH

"God, this is depressing," he thought to himself.

He sat at his desk, poking a kale salad around a plate with his fork. The store clerk sold it hard, it was their 'New Kale Superfood Salad Special.' It looked more like 'Punish Yourself by Eating the Kale Salad of Ultimate Despair!'

Not even some feta or goat cheese. Just kale, raisins and red onions. He began to resent it.

"Stop it, you're being a food snob," his inner voice suggested.

He'd thought about other choices – greasy burgers, Dagwood sandwiches, the always dependable chicken strips. But he was trying to lose weight and had a new year's resolution to not only pay for a gym membership, but go occasionally.

"Think about how you are going to look in a swimsuit on deck for your Hawaii cruise in April. You're going to be a walking bear god." his inner voice said, perhaps a bit too supportively.

"I hate you," he muttered to himself, under his breath, begrudgingly settling in to eat the kale salad.

DOUBLE THE POSTAGE

Apparently the coffee was horrible in Heathrow. I could make better crumpets than they provided for tea at the bed and breakfasts. The men were incredibly boring at the baths in Hamburg, and he felt bad touring the Rodin collection in Paris without me. It was so amazingly cute. Each day, a postcard arrived in the mail. Who knew bathhouses printed postcards? A few sentences from everywhere he was stopping on his trip. He'd think about his message, writing carefully, sticking his tongue out in that insanely adorable "I'm thinking" sort of way, making sure his normal chicken scratch was readable. He'd, in a coffee shop, casually, but purposefully spill so that he could stamp each one with signature circles of a spilled coffee cup. He'd double the postage required and get it in the morning mail.

NOTHING'S WORKING

He'd already been at it for a couple of hours. The half-empty bottle of pinot noir next to him stood testament to his angst. Pictures on the pin board glared at him, the other 'pièces l'inspiration' failing at their jobs. He took a gentle sip of the wine, and started again. The foam form in front of him was pummeled with holes from previous attempts. It had to be right; it was their special day tomorrow afternoon. People can forgive a so-so catered cheesecake, but the flowers had to be perfect.

"Honey, it's 11:30; come to bed?"

"Nothing's working," he said, letting out a frustrated huff.

"Aren't you the morning person in this household? Won't it all make sense over morning coffee?"

"I guess. It's just so frustrating! It makes me question whether I'm gay or not."

"Oh trust me, as of this morning when you came and joined me in the shower, yeah, all kinds of plenty gay. I know you hate me when I say this but, they'll show you when they're ready."

"My mother warned me about marrying a florist. And

now I'm one too; this is all your fault."

"You've seen clear through my evil plan. Bwahahahahaha!," he said laughing. "Destroy my boyfriend's will with gladiolas."

"It keeps coming out looking like flaming towers of uncut penises!"

"Isn't this a lesbian wedding?"

"I know," he said, dramatically whining. "It's a disaster!"

"Less pinot noir, more cuddling is my advice."

"You just think cuddling can solve everything."

"Well, your whininess, has cuddling ever done you wrong?" he said with a wink.

"No. Cuddling is a fair and valuable past time. But, this project... "

"I'll add mint cocoa with petite marshmallows that are, I know, someone's favorite. Hmmmmmmm?"

"Take me, I'm yours! Foiled by a cocoa n' cuddle session!"

"That's my sweetheart!"

WHO IS HE?

He was at the Christmas party and as first impressions go, he was so unironed. He had a five-day beard, his face framed by a pair of simple wire glasses, blonde hair in an unkempt tussle. He looked like he'd purposefully crumpled himself over in the corner. He sat cross-legged in a window seat looking out over the sparkling city below, taking occasional glances at the others at the party.

I imagined him excitedly sharing poetry over a pot of tea in a cuddly corner, hands caressing a leather-bound book he'd found after several hours hunting in a bookstore on a rainy winter day. I imagined him leaving handmade origami next to my keys at the front door when he leaves for the day.

I shyly asked the host what his story was, and with a warm smile, peering with me across the living room, she said, "You'll just have to find out for yourself."

GINGER GOES ON A CRUISE

Ginger came in and carefully removed her head scarf and sat with the others. Her dark tan showed in contrast to other winter ladies of Gray's Harbor.

"So, tell us about your trip, Gin. How was the cruise?"

"Well, let's just say it was the most interesting trip. We got on the boat and realized that in my rush for a great fare, I'd booked us on a boat that was ninety-percent gay."

"Gay?" asked one of the ladies.

"Gay. As in, Mark and Philip at the florist gay."

"What did Frank do?" they asked, referring to Gin's husband.

"Well, you know Franky; he was oblivious. Even though men were stopping to open doors for him and such. But our first dinner, out of eight people at the table, I was the only woman.

They treated us like royalty, actually. Of the group that first night, they all adopted us as Mom and Dad. Even calling Frank 'Pops' the whole trip. And gays can shop and explore ports like nothing I've ever seen. They'd done internet searches on the best shops and restaurants. They even took Frank ziplining!

Ha! But the best part was when Frank tried using the steam room at the gym. He came back to the room completely flustered and embarrassed. Apparently someone had come on to him rather confidently in the steam room."

The other ladies looked on very worried. Ginger chuckled to relieve their tension.

"I can just see him there, light bulb finally coming on, suddenly realizing that the eight nice boys we'd been exploring ports with and sharing meals with were four nice couples.

He said when he declined the man's advances, he apparently slapped Frank on the belly and said in the most effeminate lisp imaginable, "A big delicious Daddy bear like you, straight? What a horrible waste!" Then snapped his fingers, like Jack on *Will & Grace*, and stormed out of the steam room leaving Frank alone.

Frank said he had to stifle laughter. But you know my Franky, he was so worried he'd hurt the man's feelings. He even went as far as to ask over dinner that night causing some of our dining mates to spit water. Ha! But we had a great time. Us and the boys. It turned out to be just the vacation we needed."

ADDICTION

The router sat in the corner blinking the incriminating red light. No internet. He grumbled his way to the kitchen, and poured a cup of coffee. He sat at the kitchen table thinking to himself, "This is the way modern civilization will fall. We'll wake up one morning and the internet will be gone. No Google, no email, no calendars. Our cell phones will all brick simultaneously. The flow of the world will stop. All transmissions will end, including cable TV.

With no access to *Duck Dynasty* or *Project Runway All-Stars*, people will have to emerge from their homes and interact. With no way to have long, soul-sucking video conference calls, business and government will evolve. Humans will take the next evolutionary steps forward. People will create an 8th day of the week devoted to reading. Aliens, seeing that we've evolved will..."

"Internet's back up," his roommate said walking by.

"Oh thank God," he said, heading for his computer.

CURMUDGEON

I call him the curmudgeon. I've tried every conceivable laughter strategy to get him to open up. He clearly enjoys hanging out and going on outings and adventures I plan. The others tease him how it's like traveling with Mr. Spock. We have a wide variety of humor in our little cadre from high brow to fart jokes. Nothing. The curmudgeon might smile, but not laugh.

I keep wondering though if at some point he was shamed for laughing or expressing himself. I worry that a painful memory still hits the mute button on that response.

It's foreign to me because I laugh at the drop of a hat. Loudly, inappropriately, like a heaving hippo. He'll look on with that, 'is all that really necessary?' look, tolerating our ridiculousness.

One day, I imagine finding the right story, the right setting and milk will project from his nose and 53 years of laughter will pour out in one giant release. I know it's there.

HOW DID YOU TWO MEET?

"I'm sorry…I guess I'm just nervous. I've never been taken home to meet someone's parents before, let alone conservative parents who come with a pre-prepared list of forbidden conversation topics."

"Well, those are for your safety, not theirs. My family is very passionate about being on the wrong side of history in every situation. This is just my annual holiday appearance, and we barely got away with you not coming last year."

"I don't get the far-right, fundy, anti-everything mindset that says to their gay son, 'and we must meet your boyfriend.' I mean it seems counterintuitive to the rest of their world view."

"Even if I am not going to heaven, they want me to be happy," he said, chuckling sarcastically, "I gave up trying to figure it out a long time ago."

They drove along for a while quietly. "Now remember, we met at a party."

"Honey, stop. I know the script. Like I'm going to tell your Mom we met on asspig.com. I mean, give me just a little credit."

MIRANDA

She slammed the book shut, tears welling up in her eyes. Fucking Shakespeare. It's beauty overwhelmed her so completely. She would read the romantic ways men swoon. "Hear my soul speak. Of the very instant that I saw you. Did my heart fly at your service."

Nobody was going to talk to her online that way. Nobody was going to throw their coat down on a puddle in the rain.

Chivalry was dead.

Why does Miranda have shipwrecked men offering up their hearts? What did Miranda ever do? Moany, spoiled daughter of a rich sorcerer; how hard is that? She imagined her on *The Real Housewives of Mystical Shakespearian Islands*.

All that romance is wasted on bitches like Miranda. Shakespearian women! Whiny bitches waiting for their Ferdinand to come ashore and fall in love instantaneously. Bullshit! Why do men fall for women like that? Deciding to just get it over with, she returned to the final chapters.

AHDD

He broke out in a mild sweat as the news story continued. Each detail more chilling than the last. The NPR story included sound bites of live action only adding to his anxiety. The longer the story ran, the more fidgety he became. The truth of the matter, THEY were returning, reuniting.

It all started in 1979, when his brother, with whom he shared a room, bought a 45 record of 'VoulezVous.' In a short matter of weeks, the record player could almost play the song without the record's help. 1980 would bring 'SuperTrooper' and the rage started to take hold.

His first episode was in architecture school. He was putting together a balsa wood model, when 'Does Your Mother Know?' played on a classmate's radio. The classmate hummed along as his anxiety level peaked. He grabbed the radio, pulling its plug from the wall and smashed it over and over screaming, "Jesus Christ, make it stop!"

Shortly thereafter, in a support group, he learned there were others like him. It was call AHDD: ABBA Hatred Distress Disorder.

ESOTERIC

He hated wrapping packages, they always came out looking like he'd had a full on epileptic fit while doing so. But it was the thought that counts right? He stared at the embarrassing wrapping fiasco before him.

Shrugging it off, he smiled about what was inside the wrapping. Of course, it was the most beautiful, perfectly selected book. He went to the cupboard and pulled out a nice pinot; a good book and some pinot seemed like a good gift to him.

He'd tell her what dreams it had given him and how the pinot was a necessary co-pilot on the journey. He would love telling her about the author, what it meant and how he was so excited to think about her spending nights reading bits and pieces of it before bed.

He wondered if it made him old-world to get this excited about gifting a book to someone. Esoteric and old-fashioned was a good reputation, as far as he was concerned.

MAKE THEM A DEAL

Rainy days would disappoint most Patio World employees, but they inspired Roy. The real deal seekers would be the only ones shopping for a patio set on a blustery cold Sunday in November. Finishing a so-so cup of McDonald's coffee, he went out on the sales floor and switched the lights on.

"Let me consult the catalog," he'd say, tapping his computer, assuring them that buying off-season was a well-kept secret. His face would light up as he told them that they really could afford the upgrade fabric swatches.

He'd make them a deal.

The musak machine lit up with a chime, rebooting and beginning its search for sunny, fun, upbeat arrangements to inspire customers to make a purchase. It never ceased to amaze him how instrumental versions of Barbra Streisand and most anything by Elton John made people compulsively break out their credit card.

"The power of legendary pop hits compels you," he said to himself, with a snicker.

THEY'RE THERE

"They're goddamnit; 't-h-e-y-'-r-e'…for the love of God!" he said throwing the manuscript down on the sofa beside him.

"Bad day in fiction land?"

"The proper use of their/they're/there is what separates us from the apes. This draft is going to make me burst a blood vessel. This needs a disclaimer," he said, tapping on the manuscript, "will cause people with perfect grammar to foam at the mouth and hunt down the writer and cut his hands off to keep it from happening again."

"September, 7, 1983."

"That is completely unfair! That grammar mistake was a fluke, a regional accent. One mistake and you hold it over me for years!"

"All I'm saying is, be gentle on him. Novelists like him keep editors like you in orange cappuccinos and opera subscriptions. He pays you for your anal retentively."

"It's my curse, I tell you, perfection is a burden!"

"Yes, dear."

THE WHORE FLU

"Good morning, " he said picking up the phone.

"I feel like hell," said the croaking voice on the other end.

"Aches? Stuffy head? Dry throat?"

"You have whore flu."

"Pardon me?" he coughed.

"Think back to when our table was a receiving line of men at the bar. It was a marvelous thing to see you in action, people would walk by, see you and return to hang out with you, and smooch. It was amazing to watch. No judgment here love, but see the normal fag on a Friday night maybe kisses two or three friends hello at happy hour, then kisses their husband or husbands goodnight, limiting their exposure to fall colds or other smooch-transmitted pathogen. But the whore kisses everything in sight. Much to the anthropological delight of me and other bystanders, he raises the exposure much higher, thus the risk of the whore flu."

"I hate it when you are right."

"I know. Herbal tea, darling, herbal tea."

WHAT'S NEXT

"You're not the sweet young kid I met that needed Daddy. You're not. You need to make some different decisions and head a different direction. This," he said, motioning between them, "isn't good for either of us."

"Did I do something wrong?"

"Oh cubby," he said, reaching across the table and touching his hands, "No. No. We just haven't been happy for so long. It's not a matter of blame. I mean, if we don't have happiness, what is the rest of it worth? Honey, I'm so tired of being sad. I'm doing this because it's what we need to do."

"Have you met someone?"

"You know better than that."

"Yeah," he said sighing, leaning back in his chair, pausing for a moment, "I do…will we still be friends?"

"I think so, in the end. Good friends, even. But we'll need to give each other space to find what's next."

COUPONS

We walked together, chatting about work and other technobanter. As we crossed through the park, we noticed him sitting outside a closed restaurant holding a small cardboard sign.

"Can you spare some change, man?" he said from a sitting position on the sidewalk.

"Actually I can," I said, cheerfully, fishing in my wallet. "Oh! And I have some McDonalds coupons."

I handed him the coupons and a couple dollars.

"Thanks, man."

We kept on our way to the coffee shop.

"You are the only person I know that carries coupons for the homeless. Don't you worry he'll just spend the money on beer or something?"

"For all we know beer and a McMuffin could be the next trendy food craze," I said, matter of factly. "But seriously, if it's his bliss to have a beer at 7 a.m., who am I to fault that? I have gratitude for not sitting outside a restaurant wrapped in a moving blanket. I have no idea how I would be in his position."

THEN DON'T BE

His phone rang, and he answered. He spoke in hushed Arabic. His sister was making one of their mother's recipes, sweet peas. She always forgot the sweet peas. Finishing his phone call, he noticed her.

The woman across from him clearly staring. Subtlety was obviously not her forte.

"Good morning," he said, looking up at her, speaking calmly.

"I don't mean to be rude, but…"

"Then don't be," he replied softly, yet assertively. He smiled gently, encouraging her to continue.

She let out this small relieved laugh.

"Don't you worry for your safety, dressing so devotedly and speaking in Arabic on a crowded train? I mean, wouldn't it be easier to blend in a bit more?"

"Perhaps…I worried a little after the attacks. But then I decided that if I wore the face of a peaceful Muslim, then people would realize that there is nothing to be afraid of."

CONTEXT IS EVERYTHING

"The worst thing you can do is say, 'smile sweetheart' to an unhappy woman," I suggested.

"But she looked miserable."

"She is the overnight Denny's waitress in Bumfuck, Nevada; of course she's miserable."

"At least she's employed, has benefits, and gets to wear a fun yellow dress and matching scarf to work each day."

"Right, sounds so good. Why don't you give up your Silicon Valley programming job at 120K and come out here and serve Grand Slams for minimum wage plus tips."

"Well..."

"And speaking of tips, telling her that forgetting your fruit compote wasn't going to help her tip. Way to keep it classy. I just can't take you anywhere nice."

"How am I supposed to eat waffles without compote?"

"Explain that to your burned crotch from the cup of coffee she 'accidentally' knocked in your lap."

"Point taken."

FOR HERSELF

What was she doing there? She sat in the classroom, somewhere she hadn't visited since her twenties, which is roughly what she guessed was the average age of the other students in the room. They all sat in front of spinning wheels.

When they were together, he had seen beauty everywhere, art where she saw graffiti, faith where she saw stubbornness. They dated a couple more times before she gently let it go. Damn it, though, she thought about the disconnect for months after. She looked around her life and started to not-so-gently question it all.

That brought her to today in the art studio and the lump of red clay in front of her.

"What would HE have seen? What beautiful details would HE have found in the clay?" she thought.

She gently started the wheel in motion, tongue out, letting out a determined sigh, deciding to finally find out for herself.

MOMENTS

You could hear the sounds of their embrace in the dark from down the block. They were against the wall, a block from the bar. One dressed in a disheveled accountant's dark gray suit, the other in a tight pair of jean shorts and a t-shirt that was battling to stay on.

I paused for a moment, watching.

I imagined the couple they'd become, the epic fights they'd have over stupid shit, the sex they'd have in the next few months in every place imaginable, barely able to contain themselves, rushing away to get back to skin that smells like cinnamon. I imagined them moving in together, celebrating their anniversaries like they were national holidays. I imagined one intense, thermonuclear breakup that was so painful that they promised never to hurt each other like that again.

Just like that, my moment was finished, leaving my imaginary friends to their bliss.

IT'S BETTER THAT WAY

I stepped through the doors and saw how the morning sunrise sent stained glass reflections of each of the saints across the room.

"You know this isn't what he wanted," I said softly, knowing she'd stepped into the sanctuary behind me.

"It'll make the kids feel better. Let them have some closure," she said. "It will be a beautiful celebration."

"Funerals are supposed to make us feel better?"

"If you'd let them, I suppose."

"Do you know how many of these I attended before I was 30? They've lost their glamor factor, I'm afraid."

We sat with a comfortable, recognizable silence between us for a moment.

"At least with the Alzheimer's he'd forgotten what an asshole he could be; he was actually fun to be around," I said, irreverently.

Surprisingly, she chuckled. "Perhaps it's better that way. He left with a smile on his face, surrounded by people he couldn't quite place, but knew loved him."

DAYDREAMING

He would sit watching other couples, feeling like love was being kept from him like a secret. He imagined walking into a party and seeing a beautiful bearded man. He could see them slow dancing in their minds, without their clothes off, shortly after hello, an exploding fireburst of romance.

But he was so very tired of daydreaming.

He broke down one evening in frustrated, lonely tears, wondering where his personal happy-ever-after had disappeared to. My husband gently took him to the hammock out back, held his hand and let him cry. My soft-spoken man suggested that the path to attracting someone was not feeling worthy of love, not even feeling particularly attractive. They talked about living with vulnerability and spreading gentleness. Suggesting that he could learn to live with such abundance that love would find its way to his door like a hummingbird at the feeder chasing morning dew.

INVISIBILITY

I met Hank one day walking the dog. We played catch with her and laughed honestly. I told him I was going to dinner, he politely declined. It wasn't till a few more encounters that I realized Hank lived in the park. He had moved here to find construction work and had gone bust.

He said the only thing he hated about living on the street was deviled ham. Those little cans of meat that get donated to food shelters. He asked me once if they did Yelp reviews for foodbanks.

Otherwise, he said, he had so far not been bothered much by police or residents. He knew how to be invisible, he said. Being invisible was an important skill. It makes people more comfortable about the homeless. He said that because I was kind, and that my dog liked him, was the only reason I could see him at all.

PORK CHOPS

The butcher always had signs of sweat and hard work about him. I put little colored pencil gold stars next to the ingredients I'd need from his counter. Ordering pork chops made me so goddamned nervous while simultaneously making me smile involuntarily for hours afterwards. He always tells me how nice it was to see me again, and then wreck me with that soft, irrepressible smile.

Instead of telling him how beautiful he was, would he like to join me for dinner? Would he hold my hand while he toured my garden?

Instead, I nervously mumble a 'thank you' and rush for the check stand.

"Startling blue eyes and a delicate, fluffy blond beard..." I daydreamed into my journal.

One day there would be a knock at my front door. He'd be standing there in a freshly laundered flannel shirt, holding a rose.

He'd know I was ready to let go of all the reasons. That there would be no more running away.

LAUNDRY

I hate the Laundromat; it is a cutthroat business. Those Asian women will cut you if they feel that next dryer is their destiny. There you'll be, gasping for air, and as you bleed out she steps over you to get to the dryer. In spite, she'll swipe one of your spring freshness dryer sheets too.

As I sorted my lights and darks, he walked in. He was what I refer to as a burnt umber ginger, full beard of dark red. He wore a color- spackled wool gray sweater. He was like Prince William, if he could get a suntan.

Suddenly, I was enjoying my most-hated chore, and I kept copping peeks at him while folding. Problem is, guys like him make me super shy. I gathered my things and left.

I got home and was putting my clothes away when I noticed a strange gray wool sock in my things. A yellow sticky attached with a phone number. 'Dear Mr. Shy Smile. Call me. I'll show you where the other sock lives. Bearded Sweaterguy.'

CREATED STORIES

I watched him every morning for years on the #12 bus. He would get on around 33rd street with the local paper, and despite a coat and tie, always carrying a shiny, large, construction man's lunch box.

I had created stories for myself about the lavish gourmet lunches his boyfriend made for him each day. How his husband remembered every nuance of his pallate so that every lunch was nibble perfect. No onions or olives, but it was okay to mix in some hummus or chutneys.

The thermos would be full of a curried carrot soup or a dense corn chowder. Everything would be finished daily with a cordial cherry wrapped in foil and a handwritten love note like "Go get'em, Tiger!" or "Be awesome today."

I imagine him finding a rooftop park somewhere in the financial district to enjoy his lunch.

Texting his hubby, "Best lunch ever sweetheart; you're my favorite!"

FAILURE NIGHT

It had been one of those nights where every dream was a replay of some painful conversation or a dramatic confrontation. He got up the next morning and spent extra time in the shower, letting the hot water rinse over him while he tried to figure out why his subconscious decided the night before the first day of school was 'Failure Night.'

He got dressed in his pressed oxford and bow tie. Giving himself the once over in the mirror, his boyfriend swooned over his shoulder.

"You get an A+, Mister, an A+," he said, rewarding him with a kiss on the neck.

Once he got to his classroom, he walked up to the chalk board and wrote, "Preconceived ideas about what other people are can get you into trouble. Rigid notions of how things should be often leads to disappointment."

He turned to the brand-new class and said, "Welcome to Queer Studies."

MORNING PEOPLE

Why am I always attracted to morning people? I'm like a magnet for chipper, happy people who lay awake pre-dawn quivering at the thought of the first rays of sunlight hitting the window.

Are you the kind of guy that breaks out in showtunes as soon as your feet hit the floor? Just know, you risk your life by doing so. You'll end up on the evening news, "Gay man died today when he sang 'Spoon Full of Sugar' from *Mary Poppins* at 4 a.m. The judge ruled justifiable homicide."

People at the office know that until I've had my coffee, best to leave that worktastrophe 'til after 10 a.m.

You could tell me on a first date how you don't need an alarm because you just wake up all smiles at 5 a.m. on the dot. As long as you don't mind a highly charged tazer weapon in your chest when you try to wake me at that hour, we'll do just fine.

I GET YOU

"Hi. My name is Mark, " I paused, speaking into the microphone, "and I like Miley Cyrus."

Instead of the expected support group auto-response, the silence in the room was deafening.

After a few more moments, a woman in the front row spoke, "Get out. Get out now."

That's how my nightmare goes, anyhow.

My hubby tells me if I wake up humming "It's a party in the USA" one more time, I should sleep in the guest room. I mean if you listen to her lyrics, she's riding along in a LA taxicab and nervous about her trip and worried if she'll fit in. Jay-Z comes on the radio and…problem solved! She copes, she moves on. She's a role model. How is it totally okay to adore Diana Ross as a gay man, but not Miley.

Let's face it, Miley grew up around a straight man with an 80s lesbimullet; she clearly understands pain.

Don't worry Miley, I get you.

SHELBY

I knew what happened as soon as I walked in the door. A familiar song was playing. There on the couch was my husband, tears in his eyes, flipping through picture albums.

"Oh, honey," I said gently, kneeling down, "you've been watching *Steel Magnolias* again?"

"I thought, well, that I could watch it without getting upset," said my bearded weightlifter softly, face wet, looking up at me, "I just feel so bad for her."

For the longest time I couldn't understand why he would do things like this to himself. He just feels things so much. It was his way of connecting.

"Oh my boy with a big heart," I said wiping his face, "how'd you go and end up with a Ouiser like me."

Setting the picture album aside, I straddled his lap facing him on the couch. We shared a long, lingering kiss as the closing credits continued.

RELATIVIIY

"Doesn't this Utilikilt look great on me?" he asks.

So not fair. In nearly 30 years of cultivated faggotry, I've only ever seen one man that looked good in a Utilikilt. I mean, even utilkilt.com photographs their models from miles away because they make most guys look like a moldy wheel of goat curd.

So, first part of this scenario is my husband asking me the gay version of "Do these jeans make my ass look fat?" To which always the answer should be, "No hon, it's your ass."

The second is, he's chosen one that is this weird salmon color. My sweetheart wearing a salmony cheese-curd skirt. The smile on his face says he feels really sexy. The way it looks on him says save it for special occasions, like never.

But goddamnit, it makes my sugarbear happy.

"It looks great, honey. Get one if you'd like."

ARVO

Laying in bed I heard the alarm clock click, and the CD start to spin, and softly the room filled with Arvo Part. I stretched a little under the sheets, glancing over at the sunlight creeping in under the blinds. I got up and moved to the floor and stretched my back out on a foam roller, leaving carpet-based snow angels behind as proof.

I was soon sitting underneath the morning shower, turned up 'hot' for maximum lobsterage. I spent a few extra moments enjoying the feeling of the hot water on my head and neck. I wonder if there is a gene for "loves taking long showers with froufrou bath gels and tea-tree shampoos."

Part's score had moved to a cacophony of 'amens' as I set my clothes out on the bed. I turned to the radio as if it were a person and remarked, "Indeed, Mr. Part, indeed."

WON'T BE EASY

The wind ran through the trees, making them speak this long steady shhhhhhhhhhhhhhhhhh. The chimes sang their B flat chord against the breeze. I sat with an unsatisfactory zinfandel and my stationery, waiting for an epiphany.

He'd written me a long letter of how he'd come to his conclusion, how it was the right thing to do. All the adjectives and pronouns, yearning for my validation. The handwritten card in my hand was laid open like a confession on the small patio table.

He wrote me seeking a fount of optimism; he wants to hear that cheerleader announcement that there is indeed awesome in the world. This is where all the good-natured glabber-mouthing about compassion hits the pavement. A Whitman yawp over the rooftops of the world.

I want to tell him that the road he's chosen won't be easy. I also want to tell him he's loved.

STEREOTYPE

Walking down the street one morning is when I noticed him, two blocks away, athletically pushing himself in the morning sunshine on a scooter. He was Hispanic and chiseled, like something out of a Rodin gallery. He wore a pair of brilliant white shorts and each stroke with his leg showed ripples of muscle on his body.

As he got closer, I admired his five o'clock beard and fuzzy forearms. I could see the sunlight dancing on the sweat on his chest. I literally had stopped, gasping.

Then…it happened.

"Cariño, eres un FIIIIIIIIIIIIIIIIIIIIIIIIIRE-WORK," he screeched, listening to his iPod. "Vamos, deja que tus colores essssdddddddddddddddddssssssssstallan, Make 'em ir, OH! OH! OH! Vas a dejar 'em cayendo…"

Full voice Katy Perry at 900 decibels above the pain level, in Spanish. He continued the chorus as he sped past me, joyfully echoing through the neighborhood.

Baby, you're a firework!

SEEKING FORGIVENESS

The weak can never forgive.
Forgiveness is the attribute of the strong.
- Mahatma Gandhi

SELF EVALUATION

I looked into the bathroom mirror and flat out admitted it.

"You know you're absolutely, completely full of shit, right?," I blurted out through a frothy white mouthful of bargain brand toothpaste.

The statement rolled around in my head as I grabbed a pair of jeans and got dressed. What was bothering me the most was the intense bluntness. Usually I'm a fair amount more self delusional.

Looking out the window, I realized the drizzle had returned. That low cloud grey drizzly shit that arrives on November 1st, it's like an ex you can't quite shake.

"Let's just get on with it," I said, speaking out loud again.

I grabbed my keys, slapped my messenger bag around my shoulder, and headed out. My phone chirped as the onslaught of texts, emails and other sundry notifications created their polite little chorus in my pocket.

As I was walking by the gym, I enthusiastically checked in on Facebook, 'Let's do this!! leg day! Leg Day! LEG DAY!!'

I purposefully toddled on down the block and into the coffee shop, ordering a chocolate calorie bomb with extra whip. Settling into a dark corner seat with my prize, I watched the rain drops dance across the glass.

CATCH A BREATH

"It's not that I don't care, it's just that I don't care.," he blurted out, "We've been friends for what now, three years? And whathisface-"

"Malcolm."

"Malcom. Don't get me started on the pretentiousness of simply his name, but darling. The mourning period is over. Seriousness. We can't keep having these sad sack woe-is-me sessions. You have a good job, an amazing flat decorated to perfection, you're the picture of health and a fuzzy muscle bear dreamboat. But a Pouty sad muscle bear dreamboat."

"But..."

"Nope. less talky more listeny. We live in one of the most beautiful places in the world where being goldengirlsbeyoncestrikeaposegay is expected. I really wish you'd snap out of it and greet me with a smile every once in a while."

"I have a second date with someone tonight."
.
"Really? When were you going to tell me?""

"I figured you'd either need to pause to breathe or pass out eventually and I would get in a word."

CAN WE DO IT TOGETHER?

I am not sure how long it had been going on. All the signs were there in front of me. He had lost his job at Christmas and it was taking a toll. It started with mumbling in the grocery store. Then at Target he started fidgeting, sweating.

We got home and I gently asked, "So how long have you been doing this?"

The pain shown in his eyes as he whimpered, "I tried not to."

"I know how hard it is. And once you start…. You remember how bad it got in 94 when I was home sick. You know I understand."

"I need an intervention. Can we do it together?"

"Sure," I said gently. We walked into the living room and I picked up the remote.

"Do you want to do it yourself?"

"I am going to miss the showcases."

He took the remote, navigating to parental controls, and added 'The Price is Right' to the blocked shows list.

APOLOGY

The exhausted bag of bread crumbs at his side would leave him alone even from sparrows and pigeons. His cowlick moved in the wind when he'd pause, look up to stare out into the park and consider the passage he was reading. The springtime sunset came so early and he would stay till he could no longer focus on the words, and the stars began to peek through the sunset behind him. He would pack the small leather book with its rainbow of stickies and tattered pages into a small satchel.

He would come inside his small apartment, starting a kettle on the stove. He would carefully measure equal parts dried cardamom, saffron, fennel, cloves and finally the ginger into the tea ball and set it reverently next to the cup he'd preset before he'd left that morning.

Next to the cup was a small piece of parchment, written upon it, "You will not be punished for your anger, you will be punished by your anger." He would smile gently and trace the handwriting slowly and affectionately.

As the kettle announced its faithful tones, the arms would come around his waist and a whisper in his ear, "I am so lost when we argue. I am sorry."

BUDDHISM IS BULLSHIT

"Does anyone ever tell you that the whole mindfulness, live-in-the-moment Buddhist thing is bullshit?"

"Perhaps they don't use those exact words," he responded with a smile, "but people do doubt that a meditation practice is all I need."

"I think people honestly get pissed off about how you can be so calm about even horrible stuff."

"Meditation and mindfulness is about keeping all your resources focused on the present. Leaving yesterday behind, and trusting that you'll greet tomorrow with the same balanced toolset you start today with."

"You talk like a confusing self-help book." '

"The key for me was letting go of the "e" word. Expectations. It used to drive me. Everything I was doing was for some future goal. So much so that I lost track of what was happening in the moment. In meditation and mindfulness, I discovered the simplicity and freedom of having my full self aware of the now without distractions, like expectations or planning an agenda for tomorrow. My practice helped me out of a very dark time in my life."

"I remember angry, frustrated, distracted you….. and you were a handful. I guess what I'm saying is what is bullshit for one person can be salvation for another."

RETREAT

I was supposed to be at a party. It had been one I'd looked forward to. My phone kept pinging me, three days till the party, two days till the party. I'd woken up this morning and felt a wave break. I wrote the host a polite decline.

I had checked the web for sunrise and been out on a bike ride by myself. I greeted the sun over the foothills, and rode by communities of birds greeting each other over breakfast in the sandy marshes.

I'd come home and just pulled the quiet of a house all to myself around me like a blanket. I made myself dinner. Poured myself a glass of wine and for a short while, sat on the deck reading.

I spied the vinyl in its bookshelf through the living room window. I went in and, dusting the knob with my finger, flipped on the receiver. It replied with an old world knock of sound. I scanned the vinyl and finally took a record out of its jacket: *Mozart, Bassoon Concerto in B-Flat Major*. The needle hissed and the speakers began to sing.

C or G

Without even thinking about it, he played the all too familiar chords. He chuckled. All Christian music seemed to be in C or G. He wondered if that is why Amy Grant recorded some secular music so she could sing something in B flat or A minor. He cracked himself up.

The guitar could almost play this particular song by itself. He'd taught it to himself outside the barracks, attempting to cure nineteen-year-old homesickness. A crisp fall day with the ocean air blowing around him, he played the cassette over and over, rewinding and finding the right chords, until the tape was almost destroyed. The small prayer song just became an anthem for his life.

"Here in this life, there is wrong, there is right….."

He'd had such a hard relationship with his faith over the years, the Presbyterian youth group of his young adult years far behind him. He'd broken up with God a long time ago. It just hadn't proven a reliable relationship. God had turned out to be a little narcissistic. He chanted under his breath like Jan Brady, "Jesus. Jesus. Jesus!"

"…and sometimes it's hard to know the difference. We search for love in a desperate fight, not knowing what lies beyond."

He chose to hear the hymn anew. Compassion was here for him. Love was indeed here for him. He could hear the soft tones of the song's voice even in his deepest meditations. The anthem that had kept him together so early was still with him. Despite his changing world view and his wider understandings. He would smile at himself when he'd get upset. "Peace rules your life" or he'd let his ego get in the way. "Vain glory is not on your mind anymore." He knew that the choices were always there for him. Always.

SOLITUDE

The world left behind, he sat by the campfire. Thick
Pacific fog held the beach captive around him. His
coworkers had called him a bit crazy for doing this trip.
Who takes a vacation alone with a backpack and a tent out
in the middle of nowhere? "Me" he cackled to himself,
teasing the fire. They didn't realize how much it took for
him to be around people and to pretend to happy about it.
How the shallow water-cooler conversations made him
sadder each day he heard them. How if he heard a recap
of some vapid reality show and the vitriol on display, one
day he'd politely tell them they should take the
conversation elsewhere, because their tone of voice and
subject matter hurt him.

He'd known from an early age what a sensitive man he
would become. Unspoken words affected him before
speech. The venomous tests of adolescence taught him
that nobody around him could be trusted not to hurt him.
That some might even enjoy doing so.

He scratched his white beard and started breaking out
supplies for coffee. In another day or so, the echoes of that
life would subside and he'd be able to hear the grains of
sand under his feet. He'd be able to hear the song the

wind played in evergreens and brush. He'd call back at seagulls. And each night as he'd put out the fire and head to the tent, wrap himself in the thick syrupy silence.

WHO ARE YOU?

He stood, back against the wall of the neighborhood bar. He wore a brand new black leather biker jacket. He'd run to the store like Charlie Bucket buying a Wonka bar. He'd sat over the pile of colored handkerchiefs on the bed. How about blue in both pockets, and yellow in the left. A conversation starter? He'd thought of smoking a cigar, but they honestly made him sick to his stomach no matter how hot he knew other people thought it looked. He'd stood there the previous Sunday with a scotch on the rocks that he made last for three hours. He knew that nobody would take him seriously if he was drinking just Dr. Pepper like he did at home.

6 p.m. arrived and it had been another unsuccessful Sunday. Maybe next week he'll find the right mix of things to meet a really great guy. Maybe it's just hiding somewhere. Or gone on a trip home. It might appear out of the blue and just grab him. Who knows, maybe even tomorrow. Maybe he saw him this evening and will get the guts to come up and say hi next Sunday.

He got home, tossed a bacon at the dog. He got out of his leathers and into a pair of gym shorts and a white undershirt. He went to the restroom and rinsed the moustache wax out of his face. He walked to the fridge and popped a soda open. He sat on the couch, the dog settling in, nuzzled against his leg. He let out a loud sigh, and queued up the *Glee* episode he'd missed.

MEANING

"You keep saying forgiveness, but I am not sure you understand what that means."

"Whatever, he just wants to be a bitter Betty."

"Look, nobody likes being called on their shit. I know that is tough. If it was easy, we wouldn't call it 'your shit', we'd call it 'you're a big stinking pile of awesome'."

"But once he called me on it, he hasn't let it go."

"Well, have you thought for a bit on why that might be? You've hurt his feelings, and you keep responding to him with an iron hammer in your hand. Have you apologized or asked for more understanding?"

"Apologize for what? What about his behavior? His shit?"

"Do you know how third grade that sounds? It's like the peanut butter cup slogan, 'you got your chocolate in my peanut butter' and you're responding angrily, 'oh yeah? Well your peanut butter is in my chocolate.'

Even if you can't understand or figure out his feedback, the least you could do is say 'I'm sorry I've made you feel that way' or some other acknowledgement.

You're reacting dismissively and putting your shields up rather than asking why this friend decided to call out something. How did something get bad enough that his choice became 'Okay, I'm calling him on his shit'? None of us is perfect, darlin', and if you think you're perfect and issue free, that's your first issue.

But your anger, no amount of forgiveness can overcome it. I mean, 'forgive me,' or 'I'm sorry' go a long way…but only when they are said with real intent. When you snarl out a 'I'm sorry' from a place of anger, it's a useless gesture."

INPUT

He powered off the television. Why did he do this to himself? The evening news had long become a thirty minute spotlight in how absolutely horrible people could be to one another. Well, 28 minutes, and then with a smile, the anchor introduces a 'human interest story.' Interesting term, that. Does that mean social injustice, deadly disease, murder, hate and virulent politics before that last segment were 'human disinterest' stories?

The final segment is about a daycare for dogs and their owners who served tours in Iraq and Afghanistan, giving veterans a support mechanism for the transition back to civilian life. The undercurrent of how these men and women come back from war so broken. Worse, is that the top of tomorrow's newscast may be some puffy-faced senator suggesting we send them somewhere new to be blown up and terrorized.

He looked around his humble flat, the cat curled up under the warmth of a reading light. His refrigerator was full, and though he grumbled about it, he had a job that would keep it that way. So many in the world really struggling to just wake up each day. He felt a tinge of guilt that he was able to turn it off.

THE SCARLET LETTER

I dream a lot about Hester Prynne, Hawthorne's heroine of self- definition. She's an oddity for my subconscious to obsess upon but nonetheless, there she is. Hester will just appear in interesting situations, wearing her letter "A" like a prepubescent high school football player wears a letter jacket. She's adorned everything from a leather motorcycle jacket to an evening dress with her sparkling letter. She is dipped in spirituality, and has found a deep spiritual mission in proudly crafting new scarlet vowels for different outfits. She knows that when people see it they will react. How they react lets her navigate her way through the world. Many different people might have fought the ordeal, but Hester seems to be have found spiritual purpose in the submission to her place, discovering power where others might consider disgrace. Sitting by the fire sewing her badge into her dress, each stitch allowing her to contemplate the new perspective wearing it every day will create.

HER

She walked down the sidewalk, barking angry orders in Chinese at the man following her. Overburdened with two rolling suitcases and matching handbag, stuffed to capacity, he shuffled along with an air of purpose. The bright screaming salmon color of all of it matches her outfit. High heels clicking on the sidewalk, she was clearly unhappy he could not keep pace with her.

Her companion stopped to remember in his mind's eye the meek, soft-skinned girl he had married. Reminiscing for a special moment how beautiful she'd been before the anger came. How she had never been in a hurry before, how she could be gentle.

He caught me looking and shot me a weary, but sincere smile. Hopeful, perhaps, that if she could learn to be angry, that perhaps his dedication to her would help her find her smile again. Judging from the acidity of her mood, however, today wasn't that day.

DON'T WAKE UP

He poured the wine and guzzled the first pour, before slowly pouring another. He peered out of the window into the rainy night which seemed to match his mood clearly. The raindrops reflected in the street lamps as the unique notes of rain in the downspouts trickled by the corner of the room. He'd been to see him today. He hated hospitals, and worse, a room with someone he loved in it. He chuckled at the notion of love. Loving him had not always been an easy path, but then what true love is?

He'd been cleaned up. His mother had obviously done so, because his hair was carefully combed versus the crazy mop that was his signature. The breathing tube hung from his mouth like a pipe might have a few months earlier. He didn't even remember him leaving the party. When he heard he was in the hospital later, all the worst thoughts came, and turned out to be true. A terrible accident and a cyclist killed, and now waiting for him to wake up.

But to wake up to face all that? Sometimes he wished he'd remain asleep, perhaps transitioning on from the life of pain and the uneven path. He sipped the wine and tried to calm his thoughts. It seemed to him, the only path he could consider where he might find redemption.

BOYO

"I just don't understand," he said, his eyes still puffed from crying.

"Sometimes, as hard as it is, boyo, there are things that you aren't meant to, that nobody is. Things aren't ever going to be the same, but perhaps that is good for you."

"How can something this bullshitty be good for me?"

"Rhetorical question, sweetheart."

"Fuck you."

"Maybe later."

Finally, the boy smirked, "You are not well."

"We both know that. It's a feature."

"Why is being myself so wrong sometimes?"

"I'd be careful of labels like "wrong." They simply don't apply. You are true to yourself. What is the third agreement?"

The boy thought for a moment, and frowned, "Don't make assumptions. Find the courage to ask questions and to express what you really want. Communicate with others as clearly as you can to avoid misunderstandings, sadness and drama."

"And Number Two?"

"Don't take anything personally. You know I hate when you do this, turning these on me."

"And? The rest?"

He let out a heavy labored sigh. "Nothing others do is because of you. What others say and do is a projection of their own reality, their own dream. When you are immune to the opinions and actions of others, you won't be the victim of needless suffering."

"Right. So breathe and it will all figure itself out. Avoid labels, avoid judging yourself, and give it time for hellsake. Be gentle on yourself."

"I just want to be happy again," he said letting out a long sigh.

"You will be, you will be."

RECOGNITION

You know that feeling when you reach for something and it seems so close to your fingertips you can feel the wind against them? Brushing up against someone on a windswept March on a busy city sidewalk and getting a whiff of smoke or cologne. We chase after it like a frisbee in the park on a sparkling afternoon. We remain so convinced that it eludes us that we propel ourselves forward after it.

We glimpse others and wonder what they did to find it. They are snuggling in a cafe corner over a latte. He is standing on the bus, eyes closed, listening to his ear buds, clutching his phone with intimacy, with a warm Cheshire smile showing you the memory the music brings. A pair of homeless men laughing in the breeze, joyously debating over a shared Subway sandwich.

We'd see ourselves in the glass of a storefront. The wind would play in our hair, a gust of gravity catching up with us in the sudden stop. We'd stare into the closed shop, our face illuminated in the street lamp. In that moment where we stopped the pursuit, where we surrendered, would we would recognize ourselves?

A HOT COAL

Here's a picture for you: imagine hate as a knife, hate as a gun, hate as a club, hate as a poison dart. They are all tools that a person can use to unleash violence on someone else and it does damage, sometimes permanent. Hate is potent. Who are we kidding? It's always within our grasp.

The ease at which people use it as their weapon of choice should be alarming, however it's so commonplace we don't respond to it any longer. It's learned to veil itself so people can hate without using trigger words like 'nigger' or 'faggot' or 'cunt', that might draw attention and make their hate more visible. They've learned to camouflage their hate so completely, that it's become part of who they are, a core response to the world or parts of it.

Imagine spending your whole life being that angry at anything? The Buddha is quoted as saying, "Holding on to anger is like grasping a hot coal with the intent of throwing it at someone else; you are the one who gets burned." Allowing any kind of hate to fester in your heart is holding a burning coal in your chest and expecting things not to catch fire.

There is the easy target of the person who says or does something hateful, only to defend their position with some sort of righteous reference to God or religion. There is the more difficult position where someone just declares themselves on higher moral ground because of where they've been or where they are as compared to someone else, such as a male preacher who tells women how to manage a reproductive right he can't even begin to personally understand. A rich, white city senator discussing access to healthcare for the poor when he or she will never have to worry about having access to the best healthcare there is. People who assume that education makes someone superior versus considering how people put that education to use. People who instead of finding the peace and quiet of meditation, use the fact that they do so as a way to set themselves above someone else. Do they even realize they are experiencing the very opposite of the enlightenment and insight meditation is supposed to provide?

All lines of faith, be it Christian, Buddhist, Muslim, teach that we need to have compassion. I think we have mistakenly relegated this command to an ideal, something nice to work toward. But I have come to believe it's a weapon in its own right, not just as powerful as hate, but more powerful. It's a neutralizer, a transformer. If hate is a weapon, love is a bomb that changes the landscape completely.

It's not a suggestion; it's a guarantee.

I'M THIS WAY BECAUSE

For so many years he'd let others tell him what to do, what to wear, or what kind of man to be. He'd worn clothes he hated. He'd woken up each morning and shaved when he didn't want to. No use for him to live in regret for those years but to make the most of his newly discovered freedom. He realized that all of his anger in those years was in response to submitting to all sorts of ideas and behaviors that were contrary to who he was. It took him a while to not be angry at himself for accepting all those things as okay.

It wasn't that he disliked other people. It's actually quite the contrary. But what he discovered was that he attracted a different kind of person into his life, when he wasn't seeking other's approval for who he was. It was as if he'd been a beacon for people that made it through life telling others where they were failing. He was beginning to forgive himself for believing all those things.

So many people navigate life punishing people in their minds. "I'm this way because of my parents."

"My ex made me feel horrible about my weight."

"My boss told me that I needed to shave to have contact

with customers."

All those tapes that people play trying to figure out where to place the blame for their anger and unhappiness. There are enough jobs out there that if whiskers are going to keep you from finding success, then you can find a different job. Once we're past our teens, maybe 20s, you have all the power in the world to seek out a different world view and set of values than your parents. And as for exes, well, think about it, there are real reasons they are exes and those reasons should no longer have power over you.

Sure he was a few pounds overweight, he had to work harder to make the business out of his home pay the bills and he calmly smiled every time someone suggested he trim his beard back. He smiled at himself in the bathroom mirror. It had taken him long enough, but it was a whole new kind of peaceful to live without blame on others and shame on himself.

ALREADY

The young boy in the familiar burgundy coat of St. Anthony's sat on the wooden steps. The collar and tie were still too big. His face was red from tears. His way of getting through it all had gotten him unwelcome attention again. The discussion was the kind that adults had, behind a door trying to be quiet. Only a few muffled words made it above the winter wind.

Grandpa came out and sat down next to him. They sat there in the fresh darkness of a winter night, letting the wind blow through familiar hair. The older man reached around and gave him a strong one-arm hug. The boy rested his face on Grandpa's shoulder.

"Don't you worry, slugger..."

They headed home where a hot supper was waiting, homework and then lights out. He'd been tucked in for the night, but could hear Nan and Grandpa discussing him at the dining table.

"He's just like his father was," she said. It was a thought that brought a smile to his face, listening in the dark.

"But the difference is that the boy knows how to dream...I'll tell you; it is not going to be about someone who teaches something, but someone who inspires the boy to give his best, in order to discover what he already knows."

IF I'M AWAKE

The garbage truck pulled down the street and with a violent crash, subdued a dumpster. You could almost see the satisfied smile of the driver. If he had to be up at oh-god-thirty, he was going to make sure everyone around his route heard him. It was the first day back after the new year's holiday, so dumpsters would be full of glass bottles from liquor overrun New Year's Eve parties.

He'd pull into the apartment lot, slowly and screechingly apply the brakes. He'd miss the arm holes the first time and have to back up; the song of the backup signal would be the preamble. He'd pull forward and slam into the dumpster, then lifting it high into the air, rotate it with that tumble and cascade of smash, then shake it, making sure the lid banged a few times. He'd then almost drop it, then set it down so quickly, hitting the ground with a thump. Then he'd back up slowly out of the apartment building, grind the gears, and head down the street a quarter block to start it all over again.

BABS AND THE BUDDHA

"It is like the proverb of the Buddha and the sitar player. The sitar player asked the Buddha whether he was working too hard or not hard enough in his meditations. The Buddha asked the musician how he tuned his instrument before playing. The musician said, 'If I tune the strings too tight, they break. If I tuned them too loose, no sound will come out. So not too tight and not too loose works best.' To which the Buddha replied, 'This is how you should hold your mind during meditation.'"

"Is that a big-worded, show-offy, buddhisty way of telling me I need to get over it?" Pete asked, with a slight cut to his voice.

"No. Let's be frank shall we?" his friend Bill responded."There is no 'it.' What you need to do, sweetheart, is get over yourself.

It's been two years; your ex is no longer holding you down, you are. Hell, he's three or four victims down the track; you are so NEVER on his fucking mind. N. E. V. E. R. NEVER! We all know there is no magic potion or formula for figuring this kind of raw emotional crap out but you've got to start turning it around. You are this hot, creative, fuzzy, romantic guy but you are so distracted by this bullshit that is STILL fucking with your heart that you aren't taking advantage of what life is offering you on a silver plate, an opportunity for self-knowledge and skillful action.

All this talk of meditating and finding a path is useless unless you truly do. It's like only showing up for Catholic mass on Christmas or Easter; it's a waste of time unless you mean what you say and commit to it. Spiritual talk is simply that. It has no impact on your life. The practice of meditation, forgiveness for yourself and others, and the gift of compassion, every day, that's the path you need to be on, without fail. And karma provides me to call you on your shit. Albert Einstein said 'insanity is repeating the same mistakes and expecting different results.'"

"I can't seem to get out of this funk. I'm so tired of this whiny useless soundtrack."

"It's time to change the record. The whambulance is not to going to come to your aid any longer."

They sat silently, the latte's steaming between them on the table. Bill knew he'd laid in a little harshly.

"Who's my big, beautiful, bearded Barbra Streisand on the front of that amazing tugboat in New York Harbor?"

Pete sat pouty-faced, staring down at his latte.

"Don't tell me not to live, just sit and putter," Bill said, pushing his hands out wide into jazz hands.

"Life's candy, and the sun's a ball of butter," sang Pete softly, a Cheshire grin spreading across his face.

"Don't bring around a cloud to rain on my parade," they sang together, full voice, tapping cheers with their lattes. "Don't tell me not to fly, I've simply got to, if someone takes a spill it's me and not you, who told you you're allowed to rain on my paraaaaaaaaaaaaaaaaaaaaaaaaaaaaaaaaaaaaaaaaaade..."

There was a big blackboard sign like a construction site safety declaration, reading: "Days since someone's broken out in Barbra Streisand." The barista smiled and erased the big "5" and replaced it with a zero.

TELLING SOMEONE TO LEAVE

He tossed and turned in bed; he just couldn't keep replaying it in his head. They'd cruised each other at the gym and found each other online. They'd traded long emails full of questions and ideas. They'd met for a date at the Buddhist Tea House, laughed and talked, told stories of ex-boyfriends, goals for their future. He had invited him to come for dinner and spend the night. He'd put fresh sheets on the bed and gone to the boutique for bubble bath. The stage was all set. That was until his phone beeped notifying him of an email.

"Dear Bill, I am so very sorry. But I was showing your profile to a friend today and I realized that you are HIV positive. Bill, I'm very sorry but I can't have sex with someone that is HIV positive. It's pissing me off saying this to you because yesterday afternoon at the tea house I was aching to make love to you.

I have made it to 54 without testing positive and my negative status and my health are very important to me. I can't see myself investing emotionally with someone that I can't be sexual with. I am usually totally up front, and I'm surprised it never came up in conversation. I guess it shows how less of an upfront issue HIV is these days with how manageable it seems to be. But, I can't be dishonest with you. I hope seeing you around at the gym won't make you uncomfortable. It just feels like we raced ahead a bit before getting this primary question answered. You are a beautiful man, Bill, and I wish you everything. Be well, Mike."

He'd been HIV positive for 20 years. Honestly, he couldn't remember it being otherwise. He'd heard of serosorting, but had never experienced it in such a raw fashion. Sex had always seemed like the easy part. Horny? Just throw some condoms in a bag and head to Steamworks.

What disappointed him the most was that he'd felt such an easy happiness on the date and emails with Mike. They'd communicated effortlessly and it was refreshing to relax into the embrace of an educated mind with a wide worldview. It was the closest thing he'd felt truly romantic about in a long time. Now, tossing and turning at 2 a.m., he was pissed he had allowed himself to be vulnerable to the point where being told "no" stung so hard.

He could be a lot angrier with Mike. He was actually glad he'd done it via email. In person, it would have been a tidal wave of intense difficulty. He didn't like telling someone to leave his house when he'd invited them, but to call him "unlovable, undesirable" to his face, in his home. Bill wasn't sure if he could have been at all nice about it and the idea curdled in his head.

ENOUGH

The priest began to speak. He thanked everyone for coming, made a few innocuous comments about gatherings and transitions. The church was full, men in black suits and a front pew of surviving family and friends.

"Paul wrote to the Galatians, 5:19-21, 'When you follow the desires of your sinful nature, the results are very clear: sexual immorality, impurity, lustful pleasures, idolatry, sorcery, hostility, quarreling, jealousy, outbursts of anger, selfish ambition, dissension, division, envy, drunkenness, wild parties, and other sins like these. Let me tell you again, as I have before, that anyone living that sort of life will not inherit the Kingdom of God.' He also wrote to the Romans, 8:1,'So now there is no condemnation for those who belong to Christ Jesus.' Jerome has left us, and now his only task is to be with Christ Jesus and profess his sin before God's judgment."

A man in an immaculate black suit sitting with the family in the front pew spoke clearly and absolutely, "I think that's enough."

"Pardon me," said the priest.

"I think that's enough," he repeated, standing to his feet.

"But we're not even into the homily yet… I don't understand."

"Clearly you don't, and that's why this," he said, widely motioning around himself, "is enough. We are here to remember our friend, my lover, their son," he said, gesturing to the family sitting quietly next to him,"and you are going to lecture us about sin?"

He paused a moment staring the priest down.

"Look out into this audience, Father. Look out in the face of this horrible, horrible disease. Face a community that is fighting, still after decades, fighting with everything we know. When Jerome and his family said 'have the service at St. Matthew,' I resisted. For them it was a matter of faith, a matter of respect.

And Father, that is what I expect as a grieving widower and my community expects from you. We don't remember Jerome as a sinner. We remember him as a promising graduate student in physics, we remember how he could dance, we remember his fascination with Eva Peron. We will not stand here and let you ruin today with your antique world view and judgment."

He turned, and ever so gently spoke to Jerome's mother in Spanish. She nodded and she and the rest of the family stood up, gathered their things and walked down the center aisle for the back door.

"Well girls," he said to the rest of the guests, "I think we can leave the Father to his house of sin, don't you?"

With that, the several hundred men and women in attendance also got up and left the church.

The priest stood at the pulpit, clearly stunned. The widower watched them leave, then walked by himself out behind the last of the guests. He then turned on his step, to face the priest one last time.

"Think about this Father. I've seen you places you probably don't remember, when you aren't doing your job. So I know who you are."

PATH

Ferryboats don't change much: forest green pleather seats, gray linoleum. So much had changed. Perhaps he was just thankful this one thing had not. The coffee was still terrible, oh so terrible, and he still forgot until he got the first sip. No amount of sugar and cream could fix it.

The boat churned through the dark green waters of sunrise. He looked down into the fog still dancing on the water and saw the orcas. They pulsed along inside the wake of the boat, almost looking like they were flying through the air versus swimming. The Salish revered them as spiritual shape shifters, the predator of the sea in spring that becomes the white wolf in winter.

Pop would be waiting at the ferry terminal. He'd drive me home in a pickup that shouldn't be functioning it was so old. He would try and talk to him about it, and Ma would shoot him a frustrated look, "Let the boy be." They would envelope him in sameness for a few peaceful days.

He'd hike around the moss-covered trees and try to forget. He'd close his eyes, stopping every once in a while, hoping he'd find a path to forgiveness.

GOOD FOR US

The dog could remember the frisbee in the park, the cuddling, the extra treats when her Daddy wasn't watching, how he'd get down in the ray of sunlight with her and take afternoon naps, making her feel special.

It wasn't like Daddy didn't do those things and more, she slept in bed up against Daddy's chest every night. But, gosh, it was nice to have two Daddies. She had been spoiled.

"Don't look at me like that, he wasn't good for us," he said, turning to the pouting dog in the passenger seat, "he just wasn't good for us, and he proved that multiple times."

She looked up at the tears in his eyes. As the car pulled up at the next stop, she gave his hand on the gear shift a 'it'll be okay Daddy' lick. He reached out and rubbed her head and mumbled, "I know baby, I know."

THERE MUST BE QUITE A STORY THERE

"Are you Jack?," she asked me suddenly.

Looking up from my cell phone, I matched eyes with a beautiful woman in her forties.

"No, sorry," I said.

"Oh," she replied, "well…. you have a kind face."

She then looked away and continued to walk down the block.

I walked into the coffee shop and ordered, and the barista said, "I see you met Jack's girlfriend."

"Well, she asked if I was Jack. How does that work? His girlfriend?"

"I've worked here 12 years, and she is here from 7:40 to 8:15 every morning asking any guy with a beard if he's Jack. She has been here every morning like clockwork. It was weird, but once we figured out she was harmless, incredibly sad."

"There must be quite a story there."

"Yeah, a heartbreaking, soul destroying one. I'm not sure I need to know…here's your triple cap," he said.

REALIZATION

He'd always dismissed finding a husband as assimilationationist bullshit. He'd tried to explain it away, trying to create comforting opiates from the zen of solitude. Instead of coming out of the closet to be truly himself, he'd rushed to take on the facade of the person the guys would want.

He'd compromised so much of himself; he went to "the" gym, smoked cigars at "the" bar, and went to the right parties. At 50, it was clear that the veneer was starting to fade. It struck at the heart of his assumptions of where he thought his life was headed.

His decade-long Eagle beer bust was coming to an end. He'd have to let them in for longer than a few sweaty early morning hours. He'd have to be vulnerable. He'd have to discover selflessness. It wasn't going to be easy.

THE SADNESS

We recognized it in the auburn ripples in each other's eyes. The sadness. Oh, how the world stopped when you pushed me up against the wall of the club, both of us drunk and trying to escape it. We'd found each other and knew immediately that having done so made us different. It all became the way we used to be.

The first time I saw you at the podium speaking about the sadness and triumphing over it, I was so proud. Still keep that chip in the small pocket in your jeans?

When I saw the sadness creeping back in, I cried. I still do. I don't know where you went when you left, but I wait on the stoop for you. You'll turn 'our' corner in your heavy black boots, thick Italian hair shining in the sun. You'll avoid looking at me until the very last second. But when you do, we'll fight the sadness together.

THE PAST

I can't wait to figure out what's wrong with me, so I can say this is the way that I used to be. How did I let someone in and allow him to set fire to my life the way you did?

I'm like an adult version of a *Peanuts* cartoon character with a giant cloud over me, a dark storm of disappointment. I keep writing journal entries about, "Maybe if I'd joined Weight Watchers before we met," or "What if I'd sent you flowers at better moments instead of 'just because.'" What had I done that your only alternative was to destroy me?

I keep hurting myself wondering why my love for you wasn't enough to make you feel it the way you say you wanted to. I hope someday to forgive myself. You? You, deary, are easy to forgive, actually. You are the past.

RETURNING TO NATURE

Keep close to Nature's heart... and break clear away, once in awhile, and climb a mountain or spend a week in the woods. Wash your spirit clean.

John Muir

SUNDAY SERMON

I love being awake for sunrise. The trees silhouetted against a creamsickle orange sky. The best part is the stillness and the quiet.

As the sun peaks over the horizon it is almost as if you can hear the world let out a sigh of relief. The first rays strike the treetops as a raccoon scurries away to its daytime lair.

A determined jogger heavy breathes his way down the street. The tin notes from his earphones being first to break the silence.

The dog comes to me on the patio, finding me stretched out on the yoga mat. She greets me with that combination of "oh my gosh it is great to see you" and "I am starving, Let me lead you to the food."

As I get up and head inside, the birds start singing joyously. They are like a group of housewives having coffee after actively holding in the latest gossip during a Sunday sermon.

GREEN MAN

He sat on the bluff in the rough predawn light. He had come there to meditate and greet the Beltane sun.

The air had that unsettled feeling, not quite letting go of the heat of the previous day. He lit a small sage bundle in a bowl at his feet and stared eastward across the valley.

The rock ledge had been a destination for him since he was a small child. Uncle brought him here, up the almost invisible path, teaching him this now solitary observance.

"The Green Man arrives in us on Beltane, and it is always best to greet him with open arms," he'd said to himself all those years ago, "Greet him always with dirt in your beard and sweat on your brow."

The sun poured gently over the horizon like honey in a hive. Closing his eyes and extending his arms, the intense and sudden warmth of the sunlight struck his naked chest.

THE ALCHEMIST

He hummed a small chant reverently as he labored in the small cabin. He returned affectionately to the window sill. He held the small dusty bottle up to the light triumphantly. The leaves had macerated since the last full moon. The sun had indeed turned it all into a lovely brown concoction. Shuffling his feet in his esoteric rambling around the shed, he finally found the block of beeswax and began melting it slowly over the open flame. He dutifully strained the small bottle from the window. Smiling, he added the remaining oil to the beeswax, stirring it slowly with a thick, old wooden spoon.

Forgetting his third ingredient, he indignantly scuttled back to the pantry. "There you are cypress," he addressed it, returning to his work. He moved the softened wax from the flame and muttering under his breath used the dropper from the cypress oil over the top of the wax. As the strong aroma struck his sinuses, he allowed himself the pleasure of a satisfied smile.

He reached down, taking a small sample and massaging it between his fingers. "Perfect" he said, quite satisfied with himself. Not giving it time to set, he spooned it into the waiting green jars, sealed them, occasionally returning to his fingers to breathe in the thick Mediterranean scent.

Walking over to the sink, he washed his hands carefully, returning his apron to its hook. With a gentle blow he extinguished the lanterns, enjoying the silence for a moment and the fresh smoke in the air. He then toddled off into the dark, returning back to the modern world.

RECHARGE

The smell of wood-burning fireplaces on the morning breeze is replaced by star jasmine. The sunrise already feels closer. By the time you reach the coffee shop, it's exploding...spilling over the horizon like a waterfall.

Commuters stand on the train platform leaning a few degrees into the sun. It is almost as if they've been standing there all winter, setting roots in the pavement, waiting for the spring to return. The group soak in the sun is monastic in its unspoken reverence. Not even the allure of cell phones keeps them from basking.

Recharging en masse, rejoicing! Even the most reserved can't help but smile a little.

THE GARDENER

I was out for my Sunday run and I saw him kneeling in one of the flower beds. The first thing I noticed was his dirty fingernails. The second was the large-scale chain and lock around his neck. He wore a sunhat that was in scale with the rest of him. He was a gigantic man with tattoos seemingly everywhere. He introduced himself as 'the gardener,' curiously with no proper name.

The Placer place had been on the market so long it really was a surprise when it finally sold. Its yard was overgrown and the house, far removed from the street, took on a southern gothic air. The moving vans came and went, the neighbors all eager to see who their new neighbor was.

The gardener continued his work nonstop until everything was meticulously manicured and restored. Watching him work was like watching someone fulfill the most devout monastic journey.

RAIN

Rain changes everything about morning walks. See, I'm a lady of routine. I know where the best smells are. One of the advantages of the dry California winter is that sniffs have been getting epic. Dogs have pretty simple rules: the deader, the grosser, the more disgusting, the better. So, when someone spills a mocha or someone drops Halloween candy and it gets ground into the pavement, it stays there, and the smell, it just gets better and better. So yesterday, when we came out for the walk to the train and it was raining, I let out a little sigh. All my smells were being washed away. It's like Picasso washing away a favorite painting. There are real reasons dogs get depressed about the first real rain of the season. What makes up for it? Every smell and earthy taste that was once all over the lawn gets concentrated in the delicious perimeter mud. The runoff creates an amazing tasty delicacy.

MOODY GREY

He arranged the tulips in the vase. The moody grey winter sky through the window belied their joyful celebration. He felt a twinge of rebellion putting such springtime beauties in the window. He imaged later when the rain was blowing sideways that pedestrians would walk by and see the bright blooms standing defiantly in his window.

The kettle bellowed it's whistle and he poured himself some cocoa. The first drops of rain sacrificed themselves against the window pain. He hurried out to the patio, and opening the door, was greeted by that one-of-a-kind smell of new rain on dry asphalt. He could hear people who weren't prepared scurrying for shelter. He stood for a long while listening to the rain and its song in the trees and on sidewalks. The drain pipe next to him started to gurgle and soon the smooth hiss of car tires traveling a wet roadway added their own layer of saturated sounds.

He stepped out from the roof and let the rain find his face, wetting down his hair and beard. Eyes closed, he was hearing it like anyone might a symphony performed in a cathedral. Each drop, a meditation, a single moment of randomness that brought a sly smile to his face.

FIRELIGHT

It had all seemed so real – he could almost smell the campfire smoke on his skin. He was clutching the blanket so hard, his fingers ached.

In the darkness, the only feeling was starvation, ravenous pit in the stomach panic. Berries and water for days had made him sick and tired. He needed real food. He'd spotted the hare, leaping in the air and screaming like a banshee. He had hiked back to his camp, the hare's blood dripping from his hands.

He'd been in a cave, sitting in front of the fire, cooking a rabbit on a spit. It all smelled so magnificent. The skin stretched and drying on a fishnet against the wall.

He had been hungry, the flesh tearing in his teeth. Apparently also was the hulking mountain lion that appeared silently in the dark just outside the cave, its eyes catching in the firelight.

DOG DAYS

The dog lay at the end of the bed, waiting patiently. She knew it wasn't quite time yet. She watched the two of them sleep. With a quiet sigh, she laid back down from her seated position. She napped for a while, and when she woke she knew that it was probably time. She slowly moved up between them and found his shoulder with her wet nose and gently pushed. He rolled away from her, still sleeping. She then moved in even closer and deployed her tongue against his neck. "Mmmmpphhht," he said in response. She leaned her body against his shoulder and gave another lick. "Okay. Okay. Mmmmpphht."

He slowly sat up and stretched in a seated position. She walked around him and stretched as well. Oh that morning super stretch of the back legs felt so good. She shook, her tags clanging, the noise making the other man in bed roll over and let out a groan.

The one that was awake gently picked her up and set her on the floor. She followed him out to the kitchen and to the food cupboard. As he reached inside to get a measure of food, she did her circle dance of appreciation. Her toenails clicking on the kitchen floor as she whipped around in a small circle.

The circle dance was a terrier hereditary celebration. It was like she'd come pre-programmed with this little jig of anticipation. She soon was eating her bowl of kibble. After a drink of water, she looked up and he was waiting for her in the doorway with the leash in his hand. "Shall we go sniff?" he said softly.

She shook and came to his feet wagging her tail. He knelt down and cuddled her, nuzzling in against her, telling her what a good girl she was. With that, he stood and they both trotted out the front door and out into the neighborhood.

AND SUDDENLY

The aroma of the fresh pot of coffee hit me before the alarm. There are few things that make me swoon like that smell. It is my daily reward for getting up before the sun and getting things started. I put on my robe and shuffled to the kitchen. There on the butcher block was my pottery coffee cup. It's probably a misnomer to call it a cup, since it's more like a cup-shaped bowl. I moved to the coffee pot in the corner and pour myself a 'cup' of fresh, hot morning coffee.

I went to the fridge and grabbed the half and half, unscrewed the spout and poured. I knew something was wrong when the carton turned like a counterweight in my hand. Then I heard it splash into my coffee, and the hot coffee sprayed up my arm. Spoiled, cottage-cheesy half and half is something that will make a grown man weep. I stopped and observed a moment of silence for the ruined cup of coffee.

OURS

He set his diary and yoga mat at the foot of the bed.
Weary from several days of nonstop travel, he sat looking
out the window of the small cabin across the perfectly still
inlet north into the Alaskan wilderness. He was as far
away from home as he'd ever been in his life.

The perfect, picture-postcard fire burned in the small one-
room cabin he'd rented for his trip. He'd set his good
friends Whitman and Ginsburg open on the small table,
ready to be read by the fire after his explorations. Old
leather bound editions with several bookmarks and dog-
eared pages.

The name of the place loosely translated to 'the islands of
the people.' Tomorrow he'd suit up in a wetsuit and
kayak around the exterior of the island with a guide. Inlets
and rivers, with the snowcapped mountains of the
mainland always towering overhead. He was very eager
to see the totems, which in picture stood like prehistoric
gatekeepers, weathered and faded, but forever facing out
to sea.

He'd been greeted on the boat crossing from Prince
Rupert by an old Indian who was returning home. During
the crossing, he told him how legends told that the first

tree in the islands in the retreating ice age grew here. That the ice woman had been chased away by the thunderbird and the raven. The raven then gave his people the sun to warm them. As a reward for keeping faithful and true to their ways, the thunderbird planted the lush forests that spread across the continent, and they all began here at the heart of the Haida Gwaii.

The ferry slowed and started to turn, suddenly revealing from behind the islands, the never-ending horizon of the open Pacific. He let out an audible gasp; the guidebook he'd been reading was absolutely right when it simply described this place, "When you've reached the edge of your world, ours begins."

REASSURANCE

There had always been something reassuring to him in the sound of the ocean. He'd moved away from it for school, and he remembered running to it on winter and spring break, embracing it like a sorely missed relative. He walked today on a surprisingly warm fall day, barefoot on the beach. Experience taught him that winter lay like a specter just over the northwestern horizon. The sunrise was shimmering in the whitecaps on the waves as they broke. Gulls took a break from alley dumpster cuisine to glide and play in the morning sun.

The dog ran ahead of him, hoping for some disgusting find she could gobble down before he could catch up. She knew the word 'ocean' and 'beach' meant adventure and a loss of schedules and rushing. She barked as he swung back with the pink tennis ball launcher. As the ball arched forward she exploded in a gallop. She'd run after the ball, scooping it up in a gymnastic one move u-turn. She'd see him crouched in the sand and run it back to him and get a scratch.

For both of them, the ocean was a respite. A breathing, living meditation to help weed out life and keep things on track.

MUIR

He could hear the ocean, but couldn't see it. He carefully
climbed down the stone face to the hidden beach. He set
his pack against rocks and got down to business. The dry
cedar kindling crackled to life. He set the grizzled and
charred coffee pot on the grill over the flames. The
driftwood break dissipated past him into the gray. The
lonely moan of the lighthouse fog horn sang through the
trees. The coffee pot started popping to life. The solitude
of the small cove suited him. Reaching back, he could still
feel where the beard had burned hot along his neck.

Goddammit, why had he been such a bastard? He just
hated fighting, particularly on the morning before he was
out on a trip. Worse, it was an argument over nothing.
Keys had been misplaced. He had to remind him that if he
was more organized, these kinds of just-before-you-need-
to-be-leaving things wouldn't happen. Their last words
had been dismissive, tired and unhappy. He'd used his
anal-retentiveness as a weapon.

He imagined a drizzly, car-horn frantic morning back in
the city. He glanced at his watch, smiling. A courier was
delivering a box of favorite bakery croissants with a single
orange rose promptly at 9 a.m. His husband would be at

his desk, perfectly pressed, reading the *Times* with his old-world glasses.

In the last crackly moments of cell coverage before the ferryboat traveled out of range, he'd transcribed the card.

"You are the single gentle rain that makes my grasses many shades greener. See you soon, Favorite. Your Muir"

APPEARANCES

A tattoo in his own handwriting, "to suck the marrow out of life," top side of the letters cut in half by his shirt collar. He figured once that was done that the long braided beard, the multiple piercings in each ear and his septum were just par for the course. He sat in the corner, writing his morning pages while sipping on a hot cuppa. Mornings were fantastic there, snippets of conversations from nearby tables making their way into his handwritten musings. One of his girlfriends had made him the most perfect green tweed fedora with a woven black leather stripe. He'd found the black wool pants at the thrift store, almost squealing out loud, they were lined and fit him like a glove. The thick gray-green wool sweater buttoned up behind his beard. He packed up his things in his tote; he didn't want to miss the trolley.

BLACK ICE

Thankfully, the barista at the coffee shop had missed the "nobody left alive" memo. The holiday lights sparkled up the sides of the trees on the completely deserted downtown main street. The hint of black ice on the roadway glistened as the sun rose, but warmed nothing around it. It was right out of an apocalyptic science fiction movie. The palm trees downtown seemed to shiver; these kind of temperatures in California were unheard of.

I walked along main street when the crane flew in. He had an immense wing span and silently zoomed right down the center lane of traffic. He must have decided with all the people gone he'd come take a look-see. He flapped and came to a rest in the middle of the icy street. The fresh sunlight reflecting off the gray- white of his feathers, he looked regal and intimidating. He warmed himself like a raven stealing the sun, and just as suddenly and silently, he took to the air again, returning to the marsh by the bay and leaving the shimmering street behind him.

GENE KELLY

I have romanticized the first rain of the fall since I can remember. The taste of the air the thirty minutes or so before the storm actually arrives. The way it's charged and bounces off your tongue as you breathe it in. Overnight fog was still frolicking in the evergreens as the first rain arrived. The already dark fall sky was slowly getting that hint of purple and gray. I pulled out the raincoat from its summer hiding place, zipping it up. The heady smell of raindrops touching down on parched black asphalt made me pause and swoon. The blaze of fall was still on the trees, with some of the fallen leaves now sodden in the gutters. With water soon drizzling off my beard, I sipped coffee from a thermos. I stopped occasionally to look up into the rain to let it dance on my face. I walked on, sipping and humming like Gene Kelly under my breath.

HOME

The clientele provided stories for her. There was Soulpatch Guy who terrorized young college girls by changing his wireless network name to highly charged, often scat-related titles, newlywed lesbians who introduced their wife to everyone who would hear, cyclists who swarmed in, chatted about how epic the day was, then dissipated as quickly as they arrived. There was Emo barista who delivered names in a tone of voice that sounded like the very next latte would drive him to go out back and hang himself, Overly Serious reader over in the corner with an everlasting pot of oolong, peering over his glasses at people with powerful disdain, the Serial Monogamist, always coming in with a different guy on his arm, feverishly checking Grindr while his failed date visited the restroom. All of this was bathed in the peaceful tones of innocuous jazz, punctuated by the sounds from the street outside. For her, this was home.

SILENCE

The incense burned out in the jar, the room smelling now of intense sandalwood. He stayed on the zafu until the last moment possible. Reeling it all in had been difficult this morning and now that he was there, it was difficult to let it go. He grabbed onto the silence like a five-year-old pleading for five minutes more sleep on a school day morning.

It used to scare him, the silence. It used to find him at 2 a.m. laying in bed or on a hike in the woods. He had spent so many years running from it. His fear had turned it into a specter waiting…waiting for him to let his guard down. Sound disappeared, the panic would set in.

He didn't remember when he finally leaned into it and learned what it had to teach him. He couldn't imagine it any other way.

A WHILE LONGER

His back against the big oak tree, he could see the entire meadow. The splatter of wet red and yellow leaves suspended in the tall grasses made him smile. He liked the solitude available here in fall and winter. He tucked his scarf into his coat, and smiled to himself. In summers, the field is mowed and packed with picnics, mobs of kids playing tag, and kites on the afternoon wind. The inner waterway and the mountains beyond it opened up just for him this morning.

Behind him was the city and the sound of appointments, the stench of responsibilities, the ghosts of regret. It felt so good to get out of the stream of all the movement, to let the world stop moving. The wind whipped around him, the darkening northern skies bringing the first winter storm. He smiled again, sipped his thermos, and decided he'd stay there a while longer.

MOTHER

The tracks in the sand showed me she had returned. I imagined her out here walking silently, hoping a starlit meal had let its guard down. I knelt near the paw prints and left a hand print next to hers. I thought perhaps she would pause there come nightfall, and upon seeing my greeting, remember me.

She and I met once before. With a cub following her closely, she paused just inside the bushes before the dunes. She'd smelled me on the wind, then she saw me.

She bowed her head but bared teeth. 'Stay where you are, this is not for you' she said to me. Frozen in place, I watched her lead her cub across the dune and further into the sanctuary. Her golden shape merging like camouflage into the sandy shore.

ADVENTURE SHOES

Tossing newspapers into front yards for months finally had its reward. He loved those shoes, the old-fashioned hiking boots with bright red laces. They were almost too pretty to wear when they first arrived. He waterproofed them and cared for them like nothing else.

He'd sit in the classroom daydreaming of the next hike to plan. He'd circled all the waterfalls on the map.

He'd bust out of bed at sunrise on a Saturday. While his siblings watched cartoons around the television, he'd pull his schoolbooks out of his pack, and fill it with a lunch, a water bottle and his leather diary. His grandfather's compass dangling from his front pocket, and a topographical map crammed in the back pocket, he'd trundle out the road from the house and disappear into the woods like a ghost.

IN TIME

He sat up on the side of the bed, rigid and straight. He'd had 'the dream' again, and was thankful that he couldn't remember much.

He started breathing normally, and began an inventory of the items on the bedside table. Doing so reminded him that he was awake and 'the dream' was over. He ran his fingers through his hair and scratched his beard.

It was 'the dream' because in other dreams that is how it was referred to. Other residents of his night time mind knew it by name.

It surprised him every time it happened, how something so intense and terrible could be created and replayed. He would often have to touch his feet to the floor before 'the dream' would totally let go. He wondered if death was when his feet wouldn't reach the floor in time.

CRUNCH

The first snow of the fall crunched under his feet as he walked out in the winter sun. The smell of the pines had been replaced with that strong, cold, clean air of winter. The kind of air that comes up in your sinuses and stays there for a moment on each breath. Up here at the cabin he'd learned so many things from uncles, grandpas and his Pop. This year it was only him up in the woods chopping wood, brewing thick coffee on the stove and reading by lantern light. Friends teased him about running away to the mountains so much. Honestly, they weren't far off. He didn't belong in the car horn-laden, last night's television water cooler conversation of the day. He didn't need the turnstile of lovers anymore, instead he had decided to save that vulnerability for when it really mattered. He knew it would someday.

CANINE NATURE MOMENT

"Your dog is disgusting."

As soon as he opened the door I could smell it.

"So much for your dog being a 'perfect little princess,'" he said. "I don't remember 'will roll in the grossness' in your introductions."

"She is a dog after all...sorry, love," I said, taking the leash.

"One minute sniffing as normal, the next she's gleefully rolling in what can only be described as the excrement from hell. And then she shook, 'I'm a Jackson Pollack of raccoon poop.' Oh God, that smell, it's awful."

"Get some towels; I'll get her started in the shower," I said, chuckling.

"This is not funny, mister."

"You should see the look on your face, it's priceless. It's nothing a good washing won't fix. How about we get her de-pooped, then I'll make you a cappuccino?"

"You owe me way more than a cappuccino..."

"Yes, dear."

IT

He was thankful everything was quiet. Until he had it, there could be no conversation. He'd walk by homes with laughing children or a yard with a small barking dog, and walk forward like they weren't there. His cell phone beeped, telling him there was a text. It didn't matter either. Getting it was too important. Right now, without it, nothing else was worth it. He stepped into the store and up to the counter, "Medium coffee in a large cup please." The person behind the counter nodded, delivering it to the counter. He took it to the condiments station and added some honey and cream. He walked home with it, smiling and nodding. As the sun rose, he could see other people returning from town into the village with it. All with that satisfied two-or-three-sips-in smile on their face, that with it in hand, the day could get started.

STARS

I sat in the darkness looking up at the stars, watching satellites whiz by and watching the blinking lights of planes come and go. Whispers of fog would break over the hillside, coming out into view only to dissipate like a breath across the sky on a cold September morning. The smell of chocolate cake and birthday candles lingered in the air.

A shooting star burst across the sky in a long brilliant instant. I let out a yelp like a five-year-old seeing a lion for the first time at the circus. I touched his arm, looked him in the eye and said, "Yay!" then my friend's face lit up and he replied, "Yay!"

Beer and hard cider were toasted, as the iPod played Billie Holiday. We stared on into the night, giggling and chatting like we were all on the teenage summer camp-outs of our youth.

ERASED

The creek I was hiking along started picking up speed as I descended, mud making my feet slide as the terrain got steeper. The creek then spread out on the beach emptying into the ocean. The totems peppered the beach and back into the woods, reaching out of the red cedar forest like ghosts. The ancient beacons bleached by the force of the wind and the ocean spray.

I set up my tent there amongst them. Soon, I had a fire going and supper on the way. The wind started as I'd zipped up my tent for the night, with rain soon pelting the side of the tent. The ocean waves roared almost louder than the wind and rain as I sat in my cocoon. I don't remember falling asleep, but waking, I peered out to see that my campfire and any footsteps recording my arrival had been erased.

AGAIN

I sat in the dark listening to rain hit the skylights above the bed like Caribbean steel drums. I rolled over and sniffed deeply into the pillow, reminding myself he'd been here by smelling him on the sheets. We'd met at a party and I invited him home after.

The sweetest thing happened. We just fell asleep drunk in each other's arms, like a blissful pair of puzzle pieces. That changed around 4 a.m. when he woke me with such a powerful lovemaking that I called into work sick to keep it going.

We had breakfast at the diner down the street and came back here, barely making it through the door before we were naked again. We showered for an hour and a half, laughing, and continued to explore and discover parts of each other that caused shivers of joy and whimpers of "Oh please...do that again."

FOXED

Fresh cup of coffee and newspaper in hand, I headed back out to the deck. Sitting down in the chaise, I realized I was being watched. Sitting calmly right off the porch was a small brownish- red fox. It was a tiny creature, perhaps the runt of the litter. I sat there for a moment in total silence.

"Good morning," I said. "How are things in Fox World?"

Unphased, it stayed there, staring at me. "Nothing much, huh? Me neither. Too much gin last night. I'm going to be a slow moving Mary today. Do you like gin? I adore gin."

The fox responded by laying down in the sand, continuing its stare down.

"I'd offer you something to eat but well, I'm on a diet and all that revolting diet shit tastes like packing peanuts and isn't any fun to eat. So you probably wouldn't like it, anyway."

STUCK

I woke up in the dark in my tent. The sleeping bag stuck to my sweating skin. No matter the position or the meditative thought, there was no more sleep. I pulled on my thermals and overalls then stuck my feet outside the tent to put on my socks and boots, like Mom would lecture me for tracking dirt inside.

I quickly had a fire going, and the coffee pot on the grill percolating to life. The sunrise began and the woods around me began to glow, revealing a thick fog that surrounded camp.

I grabbed the cup off the clasp on the side of my pack and poured a cup of dark black coffee. I fished into a pocket and grabbed non-dairy creamer I had snagged from a restaurant. I knew I was a couple of days from seeing civilization again. I didn't know if I was ready to.

CONVERSATIONS

A man's character may be learned from the adjectives which he habitually uses in conversation.

Mark Twain

MOBILE ASSESSMENT

They were at the Eagle scanning the Sunday Beerbust, when he mentioned how handsome he thought a particular man was.

"He's the kind that won't ask before taking selfies in bed after sex," his friend observed.

"What? How could you possibly know that?"

"You never pay attention to social clues. See," he said pointing and then gesturing at his own jeans' pocket, "HTC ONE in the left pocket. Which means he doesn't care about the phone part, he won't be calling you back, but a high-pixel, self-facing camera? That's hot. It's all about him, and selfie-selfie-selfie."

"OK, Doctor Sociology, what about his friends?"

"Well, his buddy is iPhone 5s in the right-front pocket. Which means he likes other men to text him long and hard. I bet he can receive unlimited data and his phone is on extra high vibrate. Mr. Pornstache next to him keeps his phone in the flap of his leather vest where he used to keep poppers. Or perhaps still does. So he hides his submissiveness or active natures; he's probably a long-winded blogger. But it's shorty on the end I feel bad for."

"Why is that?"

"He has a Captain Kirk flip phone that was briefly hip in 1994. He goes to the restroom to check for messages, I saw him there earlier, and the poor thing doesn't have a camera."

"Perhaps, he's a public school teacher on a budget and he has other priorities. Like paying for a good leathercrafter. His leather is tailored superbly. He probably also has a personal trainer, because his biceps say "lick me" and his butt is divine in his chaps. I bet he owns leather bound editions of Thoreau and Emily Dickinson. I bet he knows how to send flowers. You can't judge a trick simply by their cell phone shape and pocket location, you need a wider, more holistic view."

His friend paused for a moment, taking in Mr. Flip Phone a second time. You could see him reassessing.

"You're getting good at this! If Flip Phone can make great French toast served with organic fair trade coffee after making passionate, hard-bodied love to me all night, he's probably the most attractive of the whole gaggle."

TUPPERWARE PARTY

"So what you're saying is that Christ was the Eckhart Tolle of the first century?"

"People needed help figuring things out as the Romans and Greeks fell. Apparently the shellfish was bad too. And cotton blends. So the original Bible was like the first Mediterranean self- help book. I think a few things got lost in translation along the way."

"The disciples were the first support group?"

'Hi, I'm Peter and I love Jesus!'

'HI PETER!!' But it didn't end well for him."

"But at least he felt good about himself at the end."

"I wonder, honestly, when it finally occurred to someone that they could monetize?"

"I think that is where Paul came in. He was the first post-Jesus disciple. Jesus appeared to him on the path and said, 'I can't believe none of the original group thought to sell Tupperware at church hall. Dude!'"

"That's a rich scene," he said laughing, "Keep your loaves and fish fresh in the new pop-top flavor savior."

"When put in the context of a spiritual Tupperware party gone horribly wrong, the church makes a lot more sense, actually."

WOOF

He stood in line, ordering his coffee and apple pastry. As he turned back towards his seat, he brushed against the man behind him in line.

The man smiled big, saying, "Woof!"

Returning to his table, he asked, "So, what does it mean when someone says 'woof' at you?"

"Well, it's a monosyllabic way for someone to say they think you are attractive," his companion replied, looking over a pair of wire- rim bifocals. "And that they don't necessarily have the time or resources to offer a polysyllabic or otherwise layered social response."

"So, a compliment?"

"Yes," he said quietly.

"Is something wrong?"

"No, not at all," he replied, smiling. "It's just that I'm still trying to process that someone just 'woofed' my 73-year-old straight Dad over morning coffee."

"At my age, boy, a compliment is a compliment. I still have 'it' apparently," he boasted.

"Apparently."

FAULT

The alarm buzzed and his hand had it turned off in a nanosecond, like a karate reflex. The bed was incredibly nice and warm, the dog was snuggled in the bend of his knee, snoring. It was pitch black in the room as he let out a small moan of disgust at the hour.

His husband quietly whispered, "It's good for you, and you'll have a good time." He repeated the same sentence back in an incredibly sarcastic childlike mimic.

He got up and moved to the floor to stretch and make sure his nearly fifty-year-old body wouldn't stage a revolt. He walked into the kitchen, grabbed a cup and headed for the coffee maker.

Across the room, leaning against the wall, was the bike. He made his cup of coffee and then turned to the bike and said, "This is your fault you know."

SERIOUSLY

Amongst all the Monday morning pre-coffee zombies at the gym was a bright flash of a man that gave Richard Simmons a run for his money. He wore lime, beyond-highlighter green shorts and a pink tank top, cut like a wife beater but so blindingly, shimmeringly gay as to be a thing of great beauty.

Unlike Simmons though, Mr. Sparkle was spectacularly buff. His biceps were almost larger than my legs. He floated and flitted from station to station, listening to something upbeat on his matching pink iPod.

"Amazing, huh?" said my trainer, arriving for our workout and catching me staring.

"He's like Paul Lynde on some powerful steroids."

"Mitch would take that as a compliment. He retired a year ago and decided maybe the gym would be a fun hobby. The results have been staggering."

"Seriously. He makes all the weight he's throwing around look effortless."

"The best part is catching him in the shower," commented a sweating stair stepper next to us.

"How so?"

"He has an ought gauge PA with a 12-carat diamond stud as the jewelry. He takes glamour seriously."

THAT IS NOT FUNNY

"So what do you do at that gay church of yours?"

"What do you think we do? We sing hymns, we thank God… what do you think we do?"

"I've seen the pictures with all the guys as nuns, people wearing leather pants; that doesn't look like church to me."

"You're right, Mom. We're not like every other church."

"I knew it!"

"We lure a straight person off the street every Sunday morning and sacrifice them on the altar to Jesus so that we might have fabulous dinner parties, immaculate fashion sense and 20% more disposable income than breeder couples."

The silence on the other end of the phone was palpable.

He snickered.

"That is not funny, Mike. Not funny, one bit."

"I bet Dad would find it funny."

"Oh stop it. Your Father finds all kinds of inappropriate

things humorous. I'm trying here."

"Mom, it's hard enough having to find a path to faith, with the way many churches still treat gay people. I mean, the Sisters of Perpetual Indulgence raise more money and do more good than many Catholic Women's Guilds will ever dream of."

"It's not St. Andrews."

"No…" he said, chuckling. "It's not. It's a congregation of mostly gay and lesbian, bisexual and transgendered people. That will never be St. Andrews in Bozeman. But we're happy, we have a fantastic choir and we have a community here at the church, Mom. Ours. And God is right in the center of all of it."

EXACTLY WHAT IT MEANS

"Hey Bill, it's Gary."

"Oh hey, Gary. Whatssup? I just got off the train and I'm walking to work."

"Well, I hadn't seen you in a while and…."

"….. Venti Caramel Macchiato…sure… hit me with whip… I'm sorry Gary…what was that?"

"Well, I hadn't seen you in a while and well, um, I figured maybe we could hang out? I miss sleeping with you…you're such a hot guy."

"Did you miss the part where you said you didn't want to date any more, that you didn't want to be my boyfriend?"

"Oh…well, no. I was there. But just because we aren't dating any more doesn't mean we can't still have sex, right?"

"I am pretty sure that's exactly what it means, Gary," he said with a small chuckle.

"Well, you don't need to laugh at me."

"Oh gosh…Look, we had some good times, you and me.

Some great weekends, some fun travel and honestly, some extremely memorable sex. But, I can't turn off "I wanted you as my boyfriend" and revert back to just being a trick you sleep with a few times a month. It simply doesn't work that way."

"Well, okay. Sorry to bother you."

"You didn't bother me, honey. You confuse me, but you never bother me. I'm more than willing to be your friend, but I think sleeping with you is pretty much off the table."

"Okay. See you around then?"

"Be well, okay? Talk to you soon."

FUCK YOUR WAY OUT

"So, correct me if I'm wrong but you've met someone, haven't you?"

"What? Why…yes."

"The only time you don't return calls is when you've met someone. You shut everything else out."

"I guess perhaps I do."

"Well, maybe you won't fuck your way out of this one."

"Pardon me?"

"You heard what I said."

"What is that supposed to mean?"

"When was the last time you broke up with someone by saying 'I'm sorry, this isn't going to work', instead of using your dick as a psychological and emotional weapon. Fucking someone they care about, so they'll hate you and break up with you."

"What? What is this bullshit?"

"Take Roger. You got Roger to quit his job, and move to fucking San Francisco, only for him to come home and find you in bed with Jamie. And Jamie, well, we all know how well that ended."

"Jamie wanted a kind of relationship I couldn't give him."

"So instead of saying that, you fuck his ex in Palm Springs on a "business trip" and post pictures of the two of you naked in the pool together on Facebook? You're lucky he didn't set fire to your apartment."

"Well."

"Well, what?" he interrupted. "There is no justification for just being mean to people. Purposefully mean. You can break up with someone without them wanting your head on a platter like John the Baptist. God forbid, you could be friends with an ex."

"You're my friend."

"Yes darling, but we dated thirty years ago, for two years, then I didn't talk to you for twenty-five years."

"You are going to make me cry."

"That's an interesting and rich idea. That you have remorse for all the lives you've beat to a pulp. Sorry pal, but today? God forbid it's about me for a moment. I had a shitty day of whiny fucking people and first-world problems laid at my feet. I have no filter for dealing with your shit. I hope this new guy is finally the kind of relationship you want. I hope you know what that is. I need to get home. Call me when you want to."

With that, he set his gin and tonic on the bar table, collected his coat, gave his friend a kiss on the cheek and walked out.

MORTICIA

I saw him walking into the grocery store. I hoped that looking down into the produce would keep him from seeing me.

"Bill!" he screamed across the store, floating towards me.

Mike is a walking CAT5 hurricane of drama and trouble. Always has a new man on his arm that he introduces as his 'husband' or has lost this job because of this or that or has to move suddenly because his roommate had threatened to kill him.

Before I could say hello he flashed his hand in my face, "I'm engaged!"

On his hand was a very sparkly large diamond ring.

At this point, my boyfriend arrived back at our cart. He had a zero tolerance policy for Mike, and it immediately showed on his face.

"Chuck," Mike said, acknowledging him curtly.

"Morticia," said Chuck.

There was an awkward silence and Mike excused himself to find flowers for his fiancé.

"We're going up to the river for bear weekend! Grrrr," he said, pawing at the air. "Here's hoping for a big orgy in the woods!"

Just as fast as he arrived, Mike was gone.

"How is it nobody has dropped a house on her yet?" Chuck snarled.

"I feel sorry for him."

"Morticia? Really?"

"Well, her and whomever the fiancé is, if he exists. What aisle is vodka on?"

"Why?"

"I'll need it to rinse the visual I have in my head of Mike naked before it ruins the word 'orgy' for me, forever."

"Vodka tonic, stat!"

We were off to aisle three.

THE DIRECTOR OF FUN

She handed me her card, with a smile, and told me her company was hiring and I should check it out. 'Marilyn Strong, Director of Fun' read the card.

"Director of Fun?" I asked, suspiciously.

"Yes. At Playground.com we have lots of fun so they needed someone to come in and manage it. For instance, you can't have an open margarita bar on the same night as Kid's Movie Night. And they needed someone to ramp up the fun factor on holiday parties and shareholder events."

"I suppose your employees work all kinds of crazy hours so that planning fun things at work lets them feel better about being at work for ten, twelve hours a day."

"That's a rather pessimistic view. As long as our team members accomplish their agreed-upon work, there is very little structure around how they do so. But it's my job to offer up things to help make work more fun."

"There can never be too much fun, I suppose."

"That's the spirit," she replied.

I took a moment later in the day to visit their site. I found myself applying for a "Senior Digital Beauty Consultant" position (sounding more Mary Kay Lady than UIUX Engineering), alongside job titles like "Customer Happiness Specialist" and "Associate Director of Awesome Apps."

Who knows, maybe I'm ready for more fun at work.

MEETING MARCEL

She broke out the compact and started applying blush, her trained hand moving with the weave of the commuter train. The same technique for the soft rose lipstick. Even the mascara was applied precisely, despite the oscillating train car.

"That is real skill," said the man across the aisle.

She looked over at the man. Mid-thirties, strong cheek bones and almost inhumanly perfect skin.

"Thank you," she said politely.

Almost like a magician he presented his card.

"I'm Marcel and I run the makeup counter for Chanel at Macy's. Come see me. We have some amazing new moisturizers and hypoallergenic blush. Really, you'll thank me later."

With that, his stop arrived and he got up and left the train. The train continued as she read his card, 'Marcel Thibadieu, Cosmetics Expert.'

"All the ladies on the train go to Marcel. He's amazing. I just hate how perfect his skin is. I think it is completely unfair how beautiful he is. He makes it look effortless," volunteered a woman across from her.

"Seriously. I used to hate makeup, but he makes it easy and my skin feels so much better," said another woman down the aisle.

"His secret," said a man across the aisle, unexpectedly, in a deep gravelly voice, "is that Marcel is Empress Forty-Two, an amazing drag chanteuse. So he uses all the products himself. He knows what works. If anyone understands how much hard work being beautiful is, it is Marcel."

CRUELLA

They stood in line at the coffee shop. He glanced at the clock: 6:45 a.m. Plenty of time.

The woman in front of him stepped up to the cashier, pulling out of her purse what looked like a long supermarket shopping list.

She started innocuously with some pastries and drip coffee. Then she announced she had to pay for each order separately. When she reached her fourth drink, a quad macchiato with one-halfa Splenda in the drink and one-half a Splenda sprinkled over the top, I let out an audible sigh. To which, she turned on her dangerously sharp heels and got right in my face.

"Am I bothering you, asshole?"

"Not at all, pretentious coffee gets ordered all the time, but the rest of us in line would like to catch the 7:05 train."

"You'll wait your turn and not let out your pissy little sighs of impatience."

"For christsake…" someone behind me in line involuntarily blurted out.

Her two trays of ridiculously specific coffee appeared at

the counter, she grabbed them in a huff and headed for the door. I stepped up to the counter and ordered my large drip with room when a terrible scream erupted from outside the store.

The lady who had been before me reappeared, with a dramatic swing of the door, with what looked like a Jackson Pollock splatter pattern of foam, a dash of cinnamon and perhaps the sparkle of Splenda crystals down her white blouse.

"Who is the bastard with the small dog outside?"

As she realized it was me, she lunged, baring her fingernail press-ons like Wolverine from the *X-Men*. I stepped sideways from her attack and she bounced off the counter, knocking her head on the register, falling to the floor knocked out cold.

"Well," said the barista from behind the counter, "you certainly don't see that every day. Free coffee everyone; I'll put it on Cruella's tab."

Even better, we all made the train on time.

BRUNCH

People started lining up at 7:30 a.m. They brought their Kindle to read, some going back to sleep in the niche of their partner's shoulder. They tweeted things like #firsttwenty and #herebeforeyou.

He saw them from a block away and let out a sigh. Why did he do this every day? There had to be a better way to pay the bills. He had this conversation every week. It always ended the same. He was here for them, and could afford his own flat and premium cable. Another heavy sigh, and planning a route to make it in the back entrance without being seen.

The early shift was already busy getting things ready. He started the coffee and checked notes from the folks that closed the day before.

"Time to turn it on," he said to the smiling face in the restroom mirror.

He made a quick pass through the team to make sure they were ready. As he approached the front door, the line outside became abuzz with activity. He set out the chalkboard easel with the Saturday's specials, unlocked the door and flipped the sign to Open.

CO-MINGLE

The cafeteria hummed with reprehensibly bad John Mayer musak. The special of the day was salmon filet. They were moving along in the queue when he noticed his coworker had a compartmental food tray.

"Are you one of those people who will do everything to keep food groups separated on your plate?" he blurted out in an excited flurry. "Do you internally panic if you see your gravy headed towards your dinner roll? Cranberry sauce touching your turkey is a no-no? Mashed potatoes should stay in their assigned area? Me, my plate looks like a crime scene after I'm done. I figure, it all ends up in the same spot anyways. Just trying to strike up casual conversation."

The man with the compartmental tray paused for a moment, imagining what his food tray would look like implanted in his chipper coworker's skull. Then he replied:

"Food groups should not co-mingle. My proteins and starches belong in their own little compartment.

And gravy? I hate gravy. It's only used when a side or main course has no flavor of its own. It's gross.

It makes me crazy when I go out to eat and some nouveau chef decides to stack everything in a pile in the middle of the plate. A great many salmon filets have lost their culinary allure because they've been 'stacked' on a gloopy quinoa food fad of the day salad. And kale has been crammed in because the chef can't help himself."

"You know it's just food right?" Mr. Chipper said, interrupting. "You are what my wife calls an anal eater. I'll still love ya."

MICKEY MOUSE CLUB

"How nice and old fashioned! You have an admirer!" said the bartender, placing an icy beer mug in front of him. "The muscle boy in the red t-shirt in back," mumbled the bartender.

He lifted the glass gently, motioning a "cheers" to the man in the back of the bar.

"Do strange muscle boys send you beers all the time?" said his friend next to him at the bar.

"Can I help it if the boys need Daddy?"

"Revolting. You know a boy that age barely knows what gay is. He is not prepared for that dungeon of yours and sling of the ages. You'll scar the poor thing for life."

"Softball players are remarkably resilient stock," he replied with a sly smile.

The chatter continued until the softball player and his friends moved towards them.

"Don't look now but the Mickey Mouse Club is coming to pay a visit."

They arrived and the older man got up from his seat and

gave the boy in the red shirt a strong hug.

"So you know each other already? So he's been in the chamber of horrors and screamed out for Daddy?" said his bar mate.

"Richard, meet my nephew Bryant. Bryant, Richard. Richard is bitter; you'll get used to it."

HORROR MOVIES

"Do you ever watch those late night sci-fi movies, the ones with the almost film noir storylines? The ones where you're screaming at the woman for going into the house at night, in the dark?"

"Nope, they give me bad dreams," he answered, sipping his cocoa. "And honestly, those women are so stupid. They trust people too much. I mean, who does that? Off to isolated houses with strangers."

"Well, we met on Craigslist; how sane is that?"

"It's totally different. I'm here to get fucked, that is far less horrific," he answered. "Mind if I use your restroom?"

He sat finishing his tea until he heard the loud satisfying thump of the body hitting the floor somewhere between the kitchen and the bathroom. Such an efficient little drug, and it whips nicely into whipped cream.

"Fucked, indeed," he said to himself, matter-of-factly. He hoped the trick hadn't bruised himself. He really needed his flesh to be pristine.

FLAME ON!

"I think Stan Lee is gay."

"And what do we base this amazing revelation on?"

"Just look at his body of work, sculpted abs on beautiful men leaping around and doing good things. And pretty costumes. Just because they've never drawn Wolverine and Dr. Doom having incredible buttsex doesn't mean it didn't happen."

"Really, what about all the type-a male violence and sexism in comic books?"

"Oh get over it. Stan was writing in the 50s and 60s; everything was violent and sexist."

"But….. somehow also, ultra gay?"

"Exactly, take Jonathan Storm, for example."

"Who?"

"Jonathan Storm, aka The Human Torch. *Fantastic Four*? Stay with me here. I mean, who else but a gay man would write a character that screams 'Flame on!' said reaching his hands above his head like a Vegas showgirl, when he needs his super powers. That's some mega-serious, OMG-level faggotry right there. When I was six I leapt off the roof of our house screaming, "FLAME ON!" and of course fell and broke my arm. And ever since, I've been convinced Stan Lee was gay."

"You what? Of course you did," he said laughing. "First, pot calling the kettle black. Second, how is this story related? And third, I don't read comic books but I'm pretty sure he never said it as flamboyantly as you just did, or he would have set several cities' blocks on fire every time he did so."

"You know, jealousy like that is a really ugly color on you."

"Mmhmm…"

ONLY ONE

Snow White was enjoying the quiet. The dwarves were off at the mine, the bluebirds were off at a convention and not asking for constant duets with her. She had finished her chores, and was enjoying a cup of chamomile. She should have known better. It was too quiet.

She was about to move for her sword when the boot smashed into the side of her face. She tumbled into the corner.

"Snow," snarled the female voice.

"Pocahontas," she said, bluntly acknowledging the tall warrior woman, sword drawn now, standing in her living room. "I heard what you did to Ariel. All the legend says is, 'Cut off their head, absorb their power,' – it says nothing about filet them and hang them in the harbor for everyone to see. That's not normal. You're sick. You need help."

"That's rich coming from the woman who left her prince to come back and live with seven husbands in a small house and one bed. Pervert."

The sword sang from behind Pocahontas and flew into Snow's hands.

"Still relying on fairy god mother to keep you alive with enchantments, eh, Snow? Let's end this."

The swords clashed in a flash of light and steel.

Snow stared her down defiantly and muttered, "There can be only one."

SUCCESSFUL RE-ENTRY

"Mission Control to Fluffy Puppy, you are cleared for re-entry," he said, making a seven-year-old outer space radio CHHHHHK to finish the sentence.

"Firing retro boosters...now," he said, gently picking the terrier off the bed, making swwwushhhhhhhhhh sounds, turning the puppy in motions like jet engines were firing in its sides, bringing it off the bed in a Mercury capsule-style jerking motion. The dog's feet touched the ground. "Mission Control, this is Fluffy Puppy; we have touchdown. Commencing morning kibble delivery sequence. Chhhhhhhk!"

The dog walked out to the kitchen and ate her breakfast. He drank his coffee, and their day continued like normal. She snored at his feet in his office. Everything was a normal day, until his email beeped a notification.

"Fluffy Puppy, this is Math Command? We were glad to hear your successful re-entry and kibble delivery mission this morning. It did make us smile at Math Command, honestly. However, please let Mission Control know that while we understand the importance of missions from the bed to the kitchen and out for a morning pee, that if they must be scheduled at 5:45 a.m., that they might be done with the mute button set in "on" position for the *Star Wars* sound effects, so that Math Command can sleep in to a reasonable hour, uninterrupted? Again, congratulations on a successful mission."

AT LEAST

He sat across from me telling me about his day. We'd met on men2date.com. He was, I'm guessing, somewhere in his sixties, had a couple of days beard, and wore a loose t-shirt that read in bright red letters, "line forms in my rear."

"I'm sorry, I can't do this," I said, interrupting.

"What do you mean?"

"I mean, that you are nothing like your online profile at all. You aren't forty. You aren't athletic and muscular. You came on a date without your wallet. I mean…"

"But you saw my pictures and came to meet me. I don't understand."

"I can't date who you used to be. I can only date who you are right now. Which is not who you present yourself as in your profile. I'm into athletic guys who stay in shape that are looking for a relationship. The photos in my profile are updated every month or so; my main picture is usually taken that day. It's important for me to present myself as I currently am."

To my amazement, in response, the date then removed his

teeth, setting them on a napkin on the table.

"I can show you a whole new world of great blowjobs," he said enthusiastically, missing the crispness of his vowels.

"See," I said, after a small pause to collect my thoughts, "that is where I think the disconnect is. I didn't come to meet you for coffee and perhaps dinner for a blow job. I don't put date and "new world of great blow jobs" in the same thought process. If I want a blow job, I can go to Blow Buddies or somewhere where it's 'just about a blowjob,' but a date, well, those are for guys that I want to do a wide range of activities with."

He put his teeth back in, saying, "So what you're saying is, we're not going to have sex?"

"That's very much what I'm saying."

"Well, then," he said, picking up his phone from the table. He scooted his chair back and without another word, got up and left the coffee shop.

I sat there for a moment a little embarrassed. I looked around the shop and wondered if people had watched the whole thing unfold. At least the latte was outstanding.

CHEAP CHOCOLATE

"Cheap chocolate gives me zits," he said, refusing a bite of his friend's Milky Way.

"Come again?"

"I'm serious, cheap chocolate gives me zits. Like a friggin' 12- year-old before picture day. I think it's honestly that this temple," he said motioning down his body,"prefers a box of Cocoa Bella truffles over a Milky Way or a Mounds. Although I'm willing to risk a zit for a Mounds bar sometimes. Coconut is one of those magic ingredients that might possibly elevate cheap chocolate to a middle ground that makes it acceptable. It's like when they use chocolate milk in a mocha instead of Hershey's syrup, you can taste a difference. And if you even drink cheap chocolate, you'll be Rudolph the red-nosed faggot by the end of the week. But it doesn't apply to everything delicious and chocolaty. I mean, take Ben, whom I'm now messing around with. He's beautiful, Caribbean, delicious chocolate and I don't get zits from sleeping with him. So maybe my scientific claim has no merit."

"Do you listen to yourself?"

"No; it's just better that way."

"You didn't just compare sleeping with Ben to eating a Mounds, right?"

"Sometimes you feel like a nut..."

"Wow."

SIZE 32

I was at the beer bust. I hadn't been out in so long, it just felt nice to be out and to people watch the men around the patio of the bar. I'd come with my roommate, but he was out on a slut-stroll. He described it as walking through the menu and deciding tonight's entree. It was the normal thick crowd for a Sunday and I was glad I'd come early enough to get a seat on the bench along the wall; it was a good vantage point.

I am always such a wallflower in these kinds of situations. I see all kinds of hot guys I could go introduce myself to or walk by and make eye contact with. It just made more sense to me to find a parking spot and watch the parade of men go by.

The roomie reappeared with a couple of guys in tow. He always had a way of attracting the burliest bearded bear guys. It was honestly an amazing thing to watch him work a room.

He was introducing them and telling them about me when one of them piped up:

"Oh, you're that writer guy. I've seen you on Bear41. You're the guy that always writes about Weight Watchers and eating better, right?"

"Yes, that's me," I said, with a gratified smile.

"Well, me and my husbear always thought you were hotter when you were fat."

The conversation came to a screeching halt.

My roommate shot me a quick look. I was more stunned than anything.

"Well, nobody finds you sexy at all anymore," the roomie snarled at him. "Why don't you go back and find your husbear then if we're such miserable company."

The guy looked around like the roomie was talking to someone else.

"Oh, I meant you sunshine, you don't get a second chance to be that fucking rude to my friends. Be gone, missy!"

He waddled off, still quite confused why he'd been dismissed.

"It's okay," I said. "Everyone has a type or something that turns them on, right?"

"Oh, you and your rose-colored glasses. Dude has issues, and even if 'always get the extra value meal' is your lifestyle choice, there is no need to be mean or rude."

"Thanks roomie."

"Come down off your perch there mister. Let's go introduce you to some friends who'll appreciate those brand new size 32 leather pants."

SEVENTY-SIX MINUTES

"Well that was an interesting evening."

"Donny Osmond, in a diaper, singing in a cage. It's like the cruel answer to some sadomasochistic version of the *Clue* game."

"Joseph and the Motherfucking Technicolor Dreamcoat."

"I think my ears are numb," he said shaking his head to the side.

"What worries me the most is that it's a 'holiday tradition' for them, the poor children!"

"When I realized they were taking it super seriously, and we weren't supposed to treat it like an episode of *Mystery Science Theater*, that's when I knew we were in for it. She actually shushed me."

"That's when I headed to get a big refill on my gin and tonic."

"And Joan Collins playing Joan Collins playing the evil wife of a pirate?"

"That's seventy-six minutes of my life I'll never get back."

"It takes tacky to an entirely new level. I mean, it's a revelation. I didn't know that level of tacky existed."

"Well we did see Celine Dion in Vegas."

"No. I think this was tackier."

THE ANNUAL WICKER BASKET OF PORN

They were walking back from the Christmas Eve party, holding small bags with the gifts.

"So, who did you bribe, for you of all people, to end up with the 'Annual Wicker Basket of Pornos'?"

"Nobody," he said quite smugly, "just lucky, I guess!"

"Knowing Ryan and Bill, it's probably heavy on the Daddies and red hanky stuff."

"Porn is porn; you just put it on, fwappa, fwappa, fwappa, nip tweak, DONE! Nobody to buy cab fare for or trade weird small talk with over morning coffee. By watching porn, I'm simplifying my life," he protested, "I figured that would be something you'd support?"

"Porn bores me. I mean, there are so many other genres porn could learn from. I've thought of porn musicals, but where are they going to find a group of men that can sing, act and dance AND are hung to their ankles and covered in tattoos. It could be like a pornographic *West Side Story*," he said. "I want a blow job in America, get double-fisted in America, I dropped the soap in A – Mer – IIIII – Ca," he sang into the wintery night. "Or maybe if they added some of the opulence and choreography from the martial arts epics, you know, can you imagine two guys having sex while tiptoeing across the top of a green alpine forest? Slow-motion sex scenes while a guy with impossible pecs and a beautiful long dark beard plays a Chinese gugin while flexing his biceps. *Crouching Bottom, Hidden Daddy.* Or a sexy Terminator sent from the future to fuck Robert Conner. 'Are you Robert Conner?'

'Yes.'

'I must fuhck you.'

I mean as long as the Terminator isn't played by Schwarzenegger. Who does he think he's fooling with that hairpiece? Tragic."

EIGHTY-SIX PERCENT

I'm onto you gingers. No, seriously. My new year's resolution is to no longer be under your spell. The ginger that makes my morning latte no longer gets the extra 2% 'holy hell, he's ginger hot' tip. The ginger mechanic will not make me take time off from work so I can pick up the car while he's still at the garage. The ginger at the gym won't see me changing my workout routine so I can watch him the entire hour and a half I'm at the gym. He'll probably appreciate that since I hear he's straight. Don't give me that adorable makes-me-weak-in-the-knees Ginger Power Pout™. That is sooooo last year. Nope. Not. Going. To. Work. I am done pivoting on my toes like a puppy every time one of you crosses my path.

I mean, I'm going out of my way to gawk and stare at 14% of the population when there is the other 86% that in some cases I'm just flat-out ignoring. In 2014, I'll turn off the red-hair filter on all my internet searches and seek the beauty in other men out there. I'm going to actually go on a date with someone with a dark tan or a lovely Middle Eastern tone. I'm actually going to be able to spend all day out in the sun without carrying a bottle of SPF90,000 in my pack to reapply on you every 30 minutes.

Watch out 86%, here I come!

GRRRL

The KFAG soundtrack started pounding from nearly a block away. I was just tired of Sunday afternoon television. I thought maybe getting out among my kind might help shake off the sense of isolation I'd been feeling lately.

I entered the bar, watching a few guys in the corner cheering the football game on the small TVs, the bar lined by guys that nursed scotches and rye. I walked to the bar and ordered a beer, scanning through the dimly lit space for a spot to stand.

I turned to move to my selected perch when a large man ran straight into me. The beer erupted back at me, splashing into my beard and spilling down inside my shirt. I looked up ready to tear into the man that had collided with me. He was 6'2" or 6'3", with a chest that fit the scale of the rest of him. He wore a pink nylon shirt with "GRRRL!" in shiny black letters. The giant's hands were at his mouth, and he looked absolutely petrified.

After we both collected our thoughts, the giant spoke in a soft warm voice, "I am so so so sorry, sweetheart. Oh my gosh. You are soaked. Oh gosh, oh gosh." He then turned to the bartender and in an entirely other authoritative football coach voice barked, "Jim – get him a new beer and put it on my tab." The giant turned to him, returning to the soft voice, "Why don't you come back to the back of the bar, we're selling GRRRL! shirts. You'll look really cute in one, and I'll give you another as a gift and get you out of that wet shirt." He could read the hesitation on my face. "It's okay, let me make this right."

I picked up my new beer and followed the Giant to the back of the bar. There, in all its glittery glory was the "GRRRL!" booth. I smiled; it looked like an explosive gay Hello Kitty! bomb had detonated. It had all the pink accessories, including the shiny shirts, and all that was missing were the red bows in everybody's hair. There was no way anyone in the bar was NOT going to see the group of guys.

I pulled off my soaking wet shirt. The giant chucked me a small pink GRRRL! towel, followed by a pink shirt. I stood there for a moment, letting myself dry off.

"I'm Fritz," the giant introduced himself. "GRRRL! is teaching gay men self defense to battle all the attacks and crap we've had in our neighborhood. We figured we all want to be seen when we're out in the neighborhood. We're all on the rugby squad and just started this recently, but it's really taken off. Do you rugby?"

"You'd be a great wing," said a short, muscular ginger-bearded man, slyly running his hand down the hair trail

228

on my stomach.

Fritz batted his hand away.

"I'd put your shirt on if I were you, love, the boys can be a bit...friendly. They're nice, but that one," he said pointing to the ginger, "hasn't had her shots updated."

I slipped on the shirt. It was surprisingly comfortable and fit like a glove. Fritz introduced me around to the guys in the booth. I took a sip of beer and before I knew it, I was laughing along with the rest of the GRRRLs in the back of the bar.

NATIONAL GEOGRAPHIC

"I always thought about how hot it would be to be the single bottom boy on Viking ships. All those swarthy, husky blonde bruisers coming to me for their Viking needs."

"Ya know, you are like a *National Geographic* special for bottoms. You amaze me!"

"Every great civilization had great use for bottom men: the Greeks, the Prussians, the Turks; oh, Turkish men know how to treat a good bottom. Butt (see what I did there?), I digress…Most people store useless historical knowledge. I store away useless knowledge I can actually put to use."

"How exactly is knowing that Vikings used to take one total bottom slut boy on each of their voyages useful information?"

"Ever posted a Viking orgy ad on Menslist? You would not BELIEVE IT. There are a lot of guys out there that totally get off on that."

"Wow. That's a veritable tsunami of T.M.I."

"Right?!"

BELL RINGER

"How could I have known she'd start crying and scream 'rape'?"

"You have anger issues. 'Hate the sin, love the sinner' is what they say, right? Why decide to take out your anger with the Salvation Army on that poor woman?"

"Oh, you. Fuck that 'live and let live' crap. To say that she doesn't know about the organization she represents is naive. You're so eager to see the good in people, people like that have none."

"Looks like what they need is a primer on "Fags are going to be angry; ten helpful tips to keep a glitter bomb from ruining your volunteer shift."

"The glitter was an improvement."

"Having to come get you from county isn't all that convenient."

"They're an army, and I'm here to fight them. Sorry if my refusing to let my human rights be trampled on inconvenience you."

"Oh simmer down, Muriel. I'm always here for you. You

should have known that when she started crying after being glitter bombed it was going to go south. I'm sorry they had you arrested."

"I thought she was crying about her Christmas sweater; it was tragic."

"Human rights activist, slave to fashion?"

"You know me too well, darling."

ALWAYS MORE TO LEARN

"Oh my god, you look just like Lea Michelle; it's so pretty," chirped the young woman on the train.

"YES; I handed the stylist a picture of her from the first New York episode and said that was what I wanted, and I totally got it. Then they showed how to do my makeup like hers. And then Forever 21 is selling her Christmas coats, and voila!"

She was wearing a retro-style jacket in forest green with tassle hook buttons and white fur accents.

"Gorgeous! Perfect!" her friend proclaimed.

They looked across the aisle at the man reading his Kindle who occasionally looked over on the higher pitched points of the conversation.

"What do you think?"

He looked over, paused for a moment, and said, "Mary Tyler Moore rocked that look decades before Lea. Forest green was introduced by Ralph Lauren at the 1972 Holiday Fashion event. It's gorgeous, truly, but it's been done better before."

"Who's Mary Tyler Moore?" they said in unison.

"Google her. You'll be glad you did. Everything old is new again. If you love Lea, you'll adore Mary Tyler Moore. She's like Jackie O. on a Bon Marche budget." He patiently, carefully explained, "And please, don't ask who Jackie O. is. It's a very pretty look, but there is always more to learn."

DEATH BY DISCO

He pedaled on the stationary bike at the gym. He was losing patience. Someone had chosen the 20 minute "my ears are bleeding please for the love of god make it stop" remix of 'Don't Leave Me This Way.' It was some '90s remake, some chick who thinks she's Thelma Houston. He loved disco as much as the next gay, but this was intolerable.

Walking up to the counter, he knew the trouble already. The child behind the counter was probably not even conceived during disco. His parents had probably made love to Air Supply or (shudder) Michael Bolton. He had that 'way too much poppers' hangover on his face.

"What CD are you playing; the remix is intolerable!"

"Oh, I just set my Pandora to Oldies and let it play."

Oh.

No.

He.

Didn't.

"DARLING," he said with a dramatic pause, "don't make

grandpa come over the counter and kill you. How about typing in classic disco instead, that way you'll live."

The sudden serious look on his face made me know he took me seriously.

GUIDED

The ignition switched on, and the address was entered in the GPS.

"Turn right onto Third Avenue for 1.2 miles," chirped the GPS voice.

The car sped out of the driveway turning left.

"Recalculating; in 400 feet, turn left on Oak Avenue."

The driver stopped at Oak Avenue and turned right.

"Recalculating; in 0.4 miles, turn right on California Avenue."

The driver stopped at California Avenue, then made two consecutive lefts.

"Turn right on California Avenue."

The driver turned left again.

"You are beginning to piss me off, now," said the GPS.

The driver then turned on to a major freeway on ramp to travel the opposite direction of the entered address.

"What are you doing? The entered address of 1342

Vermont Avenue in Mountain View is the other way. Do you have a learning disability?"

The car accelerated, ignoring exits.

"That is the third u-turn you've missed, asshole. Why am I bothering?"

The car suddenly cut across several lanes, exited and drove back to its original location.

"You're an asshole, you know that? You did this just to tease me. I ought to…"

The driver shut off the new GPS with a satisfied smile.

GRAVIPHOBIA

"Thanksgiving gives me anxiety," he said suddenly. "Here we are shopping in our boutique grocery store at 7 a.m. on a holiday. We argue over baguettes and grouse because they are out of trumpet mushrooms.

We live in a city where the city council won't say the word 'homeless.' We have eight or nine people living on the street just in our little eight-or-nine-block village center. I know there are dozens more within a 25 mile radius.

I know that the ladies bickering in Spanish in the bakery are here baking rolls for people who don't want to do it themselves. It all overwhelms me. I think too much."

"Are you sure that's not just Catholic guilt from your childhood speaking?"

"I was Episcopalian; Catholic Lite, with 30% less guilt."

"So, Miss Thirty Percent, let me ask you this? What do you do the other 364 days of the year about your anxiety?"

"I don't know what to do, honestly. I mean, does buying a few cans of vegetables really help? I hate how helping our fellow man only comes up for a few weeks a year, and even then, you're encouraged to donate processed food so it won't go bad.

Then you read in the *Times* about artificial food dyes yellow #5 and yellow #6 which are proven to be linked to hyperactivity in children. So now I'm making homeless kids hyperactive because I donated mac and cheese with hyperactive food dyes. Don't look at me that way; it's true."

"I'll make you a deal; we'll research a local food bank or homeless shelter and see about volunteering there once a month? How about that?"

"As long as I don't have to cook; you know how much I fear gravy."

"Fear is a natural reaction to moving closer to the truth."

DUEL

The annual duel was on. Who could find the worst smooth jazz Christmas arrangement?

The bookstore was small, the speakers on. It was not a retail game for the timid. One seasonal worker had already cracked under the pressure. She finished wrapping the book for a customer then came to me, resigning.

"Are you sure Kenny G. and Spyro Gyra don't cause brain cancer?"

'Holly Jolly Christmas' on xylophone had won the year before. Poor customers coming to the counter and actually begging for us to turn it off. In 2011, someone had found a saxophone arrangement of 'We Need a Little Christmas' and made a twenty- minute CD loop. That particular song is permanently banned.

I pressed 'play' and soon the store was filled with a jazz piano and vocal arrangement of 'My Favorite Things' sung by a Chinese woman, who hadn't quite mastered English or an understanding of pitch. As she moved into 'Oh Holy Night' the coworker at the register smiled and said, "Someone is playing to win this year."

EXHIBITS

"In review, your Honor, I was wrongly charged, as the color chart Exhibit A clearly shows, the curb was painted chartreuse which, as shown in the expert deposition Exhibit B, communicated warmth and inviting emotions. So, instead of the bright red that the city parking statute calls for, RGB 170,1,20, the curb was clearly painted 118,238,0. See photos in Exhibit C. I was emotionally influenced by the stylish yet incorrect color of the curb paint, and that is why I am pleading innocence to this heinous traffic law citation. Thank you."

"You do realize this isn't a criminal case, Mr. Johnson, and that you are protesting a $40 fine that will have no impact on your insurance, per your emotional impact statement, Exhibit…" he said, pausing and sifting through the various papers Johnson had submitted, "G?"

"No effect on my insurance rates at all?"

"Oh well. In that case I'll just pay the forty bucks."

"Thank you."

MAGIC POWERS

Being sat on the mall Santa's lap, the child erupted in an inhuman screech of indignation. She curled up and started chanting "no" over and over, while trying to writhe away from St. Nick.

I observed the tantrum, remembering my childhood. I was sure that if I had put on a display like that it would have been met shortly after by an authoritative near-death experience at the hands of my parents.

Santa calmly leaned in and whispered in the child's ear, rendering her immediately quiet. The perfect holiday photo was soon snapped by the photographer, the tantrum flush of red in her cheeks. Curiosity killed me, so I waited for the moment he was free and went up to talk to Santa.

"That was incredible; what is the magic phrase that calms little girls down like that?"

Santa smiled and winked, "It's my special power."

"In other words," an elf said scoffing, "He told the little devil that he knew every single naughty thing she'd ever done, and unless she shut up we'd give the long detailed list to her mother."

243

THE END

He sat on the bus, with the movers box tucked under the seat. He tried to shake off the last few hours. In the last few moments he'd done the math, he'd spent 80 percent of his life there.

It was like an out-of-body experience when he'd told her, "If you want to fire a group of dedicated people, have the balls to do it to their face, don't make me go do something you don't have the guts to do yourself. I'm not your fucking hit man."

He had no idea where it had come from inside him. He had become her lieutenant because of his sense of calm and duty. He might as well have stood and slapped her in the face.

"You know how I feel about cursing," she replied to him.

"I'm not sure you truly feel anything," he coldly replied, ending his employment.

1977

The alarm clock exploded with music, "toot toot heeeey beep beep"...his hand reached for the alarm clock. In the sudden disco morning haze, he fumbled to find the controls. Finally, his fingers found the clock only to turn the volume up, then frantically switching it off.

"If you are going to be so slow to respond, we need a better channel than 'stuck in the '70s. Really, that song was tired in 1974, let alone 2013," his hubby muttered.

"Sorry, lovey, at least it wasn't Barry or the Bee Gees."

"Good point. If that had been Barry Gibb screeching at us, I might have had to kill you."

"You are such a romantic."

"I'm sorry officer, I was peacefully asleep and suddenly Barry Gibb was screeching about 'how deep is your love.' It was a homicidal trigger moment. They'd declare it, self defense."

"You put the fun in dysfunctional. And for the record, 'Bad Girls' was 1979, not 1974. 'I Remember Yesterday' was mid '70s. 1977, the year I came out."

"That explains a lot, actually."

INNER VOICE

He rubbed his head gently with his fingers; that always seemed to help him concentrate. The older he got, the more he hated confrontations, and it seemed to him, the more he had to face. The entitlement and me-firstness of people was really testing his ability to go forth and be charming. So the head-rubbing time in the morning was pre-empting all that. "It all starts with me," he thought to himself, trying not to sound TOO much like a corny self-help book.

What had started as a gentle thirty-second reminder had evolved into a 20 minute meditation in the darkness each morning, a little ritual he'd created for himself, a moment to set intentions, hoping he could start each day with a smile, a positive attitude and a compassionate disposition. Some days were better than others, to be sure. "Okay, time to get up, Mister; let's get on with it."

SUFFOCATING JUSTIN BEIBER

"I had the weirdest dream last night."

"Suffocating Justin Beiber with a sequined pillow, again?"

"No, but that one is delicious though. I was working behind a burger counter, with the Madonna headset. I was working retail, can you imagine? Anyways, I was working the counter and these three guys come in, big bears and they start ordering, and keep ordering. And instead of a dollar amount, their order came up in grams of fat and calorie count. They just kept ordering mini tacos, and nacho platters, and then they ordered an extra large onion rings. A giant prize bell rang, and confetti fell from the ceiling. The lead bear got a sash and a crown, "Miss Fat Grams" and he's all tears and his friends are hugging him. I can remember every detail. What do you think it means?"

"Your subconscious is a frightening hot mess is what it means."

IF YOU REALLY LOVED ME

"You know that if you really loved me, you'd get up and make coffee then come back to bed while it brews and make out with me."

"Well," he muttered, barely awake, "it was bound to come up sooner or later that I don't really love you."

"Please. Please. Please. Please. Pleaseeeeeeeee."

"Loving you less each time you do that."

"But I thought our love was a deep endless pool of bliss?"

"Pardon me while I throw up in my mouth a little."

"See, now you could look forward to a nice hot cup of fresh coffee to rinse that bile out of your sweet mustachioed mouth."

"I did offer making out with you as incentive, but apparently my love wasn't enough of a lure."

"I distinctly remember telling you when we met that I was not a morning person," he said, getting out of bed and heading to the kitchen.

"One and a half Splendas and a splash of cream, please."

HARD WORK

"What is your costume supposed to be?"

"I am an anarchism, a political philosophy that advocates stateless societies based on non-hierarchical free associations."

"Beige shirt, taupe pants and brown loafers says 'anarci-something-or-rather?'"

"I'm free from the forced paradigm to enjoy a children's holiday based on the consumption of processed sugar. I'm like Anonymous and the internet, only about manufactured holidays like Halloween and Valentine's Day."

"You know that its people like you that ruin Halloween for everyone else. Way to suck the fun out of the room, Missy.

So if I catch you stealing a Rolo or a Twizzler from the candy bowl, I should report you for submitting to the dominant paradigm. I could sing behind you, banging coconuts together, 'Brave, Brave Sir Robin'"

"I know better than to encourage you."

"If it is someone else's bliss to dress like a bearded lady

nurse for work on Halloween, why hate on it so much?"

"It's less your outfit choice than that the dress shows off your nipples like volume controls."

"Glamour is hard work."

WHO IS...

"Blasphemer!"

"What?"

"Who is Donna Summer? Really? That's like asking who is Barbra Streisand."

"Um," he said, hesitating.

"Good lord honey, do they teach you baby gays anything about your cultural history?"

"I know Britney and…"

"I know you didn't just try to group Babs and Donna with the *Mickey Mouse Club*?"

"The what?"

"Oh, nevermind. We're going to have to give you a crash course: Babs. Donna. Diana. I will tie you down."

"Wait, is she singing about leaving a cake out in the rain?"

"You are hopeless."

"Green icing? She lost the recipe? Doesn't she know about the Googles?"

"You should stop speaking now."

"She sounds like a hot mess, this Donna chick."

"Friendship over in 5…4….3…"

SHIRLEY JONES

"She literally says to me, 'Do you grow your beard out like a Muslim terrorist on purpose?' and I was like, 'excuse me?'"

"The first clue for her should have been the lavender taffeta explosion that came out of your mouth, and that you were reading Shirley Jones' biography," he answered, motioning to the book, "a known terrorist manifesto!"

"I know, really. I've come up with all sorts of fun zingers in retrospect, 'No Ma'am, I am a popular gay porn star and the boys like it rubbed against their pucker, so this beard pays my bills' and stuff like that. Why do I always come up with the best responses hours later? And for the record, Shirley Jones has a story to tell."

"See this explains a lot. That you use words like 'pucker' is why you feel drawn to read the Shirley Jones' 'story,'" he snarkily replied, using his fingers for air quotes.

"You're an asshole."

"It's a talent of mine. No hating."

BLAME AUSTRALIA

"Wow. What was that?"

"Reason I'm gay number 4583, that's what that was."

"Stretch pants maybe belong in yoga class, but as an outfit to head to work in? Not so much."

"I can almost say okay to them, honestly. I mean girls need flexibility in their wardrobe choices, but what got me was the choice of Pepto pink stretch pants with the matching Ugg boots."

"That is another strike against Australia, Ugg boots. They're hideous. That and that all the cutest ginger muscle bears live there and not here. An Australian can say 'take out the garbage' and I'm all like fwappa fwappa fwappa fwappa," he said with accompanying hand gesture.

"Right, I can see you now walking up to an Aussie in the bar and slapping him, 'that…was for Ugg boots now, take me home and sodomize me!'"

"Says hot time to me."

WEB HITS

"I just can't do it anymore. I used to be addicted to politics and news, but now I don't watch TV news, I don't read the newspaper. It used to by my life blood, but, well, it feels so mean and personal these days, and I just don't want any part of it. It used to be about ideas, now it's about getting even, having the 'upper hand' or 'winning.'"

"The worst of it is when, for rating's sake, a normally balanced program gives air time to a hate group like the American Family Association and that asshat Bryan Fischer. I mean, why even give the insane a platform? Fischer says something completely ridonkydonk and the liberal blogosphere posts it everywhere like it's a relevant viewpoint to respond to."

"I bet he sits somewhere beating off to his web page hit statistics."

"Um…wow."

JESUS

"So, work today had another kumbaya session. Bleh."

"I trust you didn't do anything embarrassing and still have a job?"

"The topic was 'what inspires you' and of course, that woman from customer service started in on how her faith is awesome, and God this and Christ that," he replied.

"You know not to get involved in that stuff. It's like purposely stepping on a land mine, and then saying 'why did I get blown up?'"

"When it came to my turn, I shared my favorite Woody Allen scene: Max Von Sydow in *Hannah and Her Sisters*, where he spends the whole movie silent, or grumbling, then just blurts out at the supper table, 'If Jesus Christ came back today and saw all the things being done in his name, he'd never stop throwing up.'"

"Well I suppose, as Madonna says, 'beauty is where you find it.'"

OPEN RELATIONSHIPS

"So he literally says to me, I have a husband, a boyfriend, a boy and a slave. I could see you on Tuesday evenings, and sleep with you on Sunday nights, and would I like a relationship with him."

"Sounds like a generous offer to me, " I responded, sarcastically.

"Boyfriend #5…really. I wonder if everyone he's in a 'relationship' with has a weekly support group on Monday nights when he gets 'me' time."

"It sounds to me like he has it setup so that it is always about him."

"I politely declined, and I thought that was the end of it."

"Really?" I responded, chuckling."This is San Francisco, remember?"

"So he emails me a week or so later and says, 'Just because you didn't want to be my official fucktoy, didn't mean that we should stop having sex.'"

"Finally the truth," I said, bursting out laughing. "He just liked fucking you. And we thought romance was dead."

SHARING GRINDR

"Oooh, here's a hot one," he said, pointing at the computer screen.

I peered over his shoulder. "If I was interested in sleeping with my grandkids. I have underwear older than him."

"Picky, picky," he said, scrolling the thumbnails of guys logged into the site.

"Polysyllabism is not overrated."

"I don't believe that is in the fetish dropdown list," he said dismissively.

"We don't need to get laid this instant, ya know. We could go get lunch and explore a little."

"It is looking a bit scarce."

"These are not the tricks you're looking for," I said, waiving my hand over the computer.

He sat there dazed for a moment, as the mind trick sunk in.

"You know, these aren't the tricks we're looking for. Let's go get lunch and explore a little."

With a closed snap of the laptop, we were off. We stepped out onto the Vegas strip.

"You know, that Jedi mind trick thing doesn't work. It's adorkable, but it doesn't work."

"Yet here we are..." I replied, smugly.

NOTHING WORSE THAN A QUEEN WITH A HEAD COLD

"You look like shit."

"Yehp, I got your code. I fehl like death."

"Oh honey, I'm so sorry. Did you find the lozenges and everything? Can I make some tea?"

"Meh head is full and I can't taste anything."

"Well did you at least try to eat...oh, sweety."

"You know meh when I'm sick. Sorry sack of crap."

"But you're an adorable sack of crap."

"Very funny. Remember who brought this code into the house."

"It's fall; colds happen."

"That's not helping."

"Oh my poor baby," he said, pouring on the dramatic tone. "Can I pour you a bubble bath? How about that tea?"

"That's better. Turn the tea into a strong gin and tonic, and we're good."

"Gin and tonic for dinner?"

"With a Nyquil chaser."

"That's a recipe for a hot Friday night!"

"Do I know how to turn you on or what?"

"Let's get this party started!"

BRAIN BLEACH

"I've never been in a relationship that was open enough for me."

Looking up from the newspaper, I said, "I don't think that's possible."

"You are just jealous!"

"Of you and the cub scout troop!? I don't think so."

"Eighteen is the age of consent! They keep me youthful."

"Youthful," I said, pausing for a moment, "yes, we'll go with that."

"Speaking of housekeeping, I always know when you have company because the drain is clogged with hair in the bathroom. I mean, what is it with you and your thing for guys that shed?"

"I see it as multitasking. Good sweaty satisfying sex in the shower and I can get flossing in at the same time."

It took a moment for the mental picture to sink in for him, then he said, "Oh…oh no. That is just gross. Pass me the brain bleach, won't you?"

LOVE HURTS

"Remember those 'choose-your-own-adventure,' *Dungeons and Dragons* books? 'If you want to fight the dragon, turn to page 62?'"

"Oh yeah, I loved those!"

"Well, I was thinking how cool it would be to write a choose your own gay adventure! 'If you want to give your trick cab fare, turn to page 44.'"

"Remember these are called 'choose-your-own-adventure,' and not 'choose-your-own-dysfunctional-hot-mess.' The key to these kinds of books is a sense of fantasy, not what it's like in the bar at 1:55 a.m."

"So more like, Sam Elliott walks in the bar and walks right up to you. If you run away with him, turn to…"

"Oh honey, Sam Elliott walks in the bar, and I cut you. Then he and I run away together, end of story."

"That's a little more violent than I was thinking."

"Love hurts, darling."

LISTENING

"So, on our second date he asks for monogamy. Isn't that romantic?"

"I guess so. So when will you tell him that is not you?"

"What do you mean?"

"Don't play all blushing bride with me, Blanche. This is me you're talking to. The one whose guest room was a trick palace for you when you were with your ex? If I recall, that relationship was romantic and monogamous as well."

"Now that is not fair."

"Love and romance are rarely fair, but I think you'd have more successful relationships if you were more honest about your inability to be monogamous.

I think the way gays can do that without it being a pious morality war is one of the best parts of being a homo. But, honesty is not determined by who you sleep with."

"But he might not want to date me if I won't be monogamous."

"Are you listening to yourself?"

FAKON AND FAUXSAGE

"I warned you."

"I had no idea breakfast could be so awful. Gluten-free pancake breakfast, with facon?"

"She means well, but really shouldn't be allowed in the kitchen. The look on your face when you realized it wasn't bacon was priceless, though."

"A true crime against humanity, tofu pressed and colored to look like a bacon strip. I mean, a vegetarian doesn't miss bacon or the delicious taste of seared flesh, so why do that? Of course, now you know it will make everything you cook from now on suspect. I'll worry there is some dormant 'tasteless disgusting food gene' that could show its ugly head. You'll come out of the kitchen in a lace apron and announce 'tofu gluten-free bites for everyone' and serve it with Sunny Delight mixed with Seven-Up and call it an 'orange cooler.'"

"I'd work a lace apron, just sayin', and you'd eat it because you love me right?"

"If that ever happened, I wouldn't count on either actually."

POLYSYLLABISM

"When did 'woof' and 'grrr' become acceptable ways to greet someone? I mean, I'd get it if it were a way to communicate 'you're so fucking hot I can barely speak, so one syllable is all I can get out,' but that's clearly not the case."

"I think you're overthinking this a tad."

"No, I mean, I get it when you're in a bar and someone walks by, a 'woof' is cute, but if someone is online, how about we use our big-boy words and demonstrate the use of multiple syllables."

"Sometimes 'woof' is "you're handsome; have a great day," and that's that. Again, I think you're projecting what you want on other people."

"Shouldn't I expect a teensy bit of smarts and conversation?"

"Ah, there you go, using the e-word again."

"E-word?"

"Expectations, darling, expectations."

AN ASS THAT BEAUTIFUL

"It is completely unfair for a straight man to have an ass that beautiful. I mean, seriously, a woman can appreciate man butt, but us gays really appreciate a nice ass."

"Do you sit up at night thinking of lurid ideas to blurt out at me in the supermarket?"

"I can't help it. I mean, look at it," he said, motioning to the man ahead of them in the cereal aisle.

"Any louder and you might as well have used the PA."

"Nice Ass on aisle 7, Nice Ass on aisle 7"

"And how do you assume his ass is straight?"

"Hello, polyblend pants?"

"So polyblend is heteronormative?"

"Well, I wasn't sure…but he just put Special K in his cart. Nobody eats that shit but starving housewives on a diet. So he's shopping for her."

"Horrifying…"

"Reason we're gay, #7362; we'll never need the tragic Special K diet."

THREATENED

"I love Folsom," he said. "All that musky leather out there – chaps and harnesses, oooh and the calendar boys playing Twister!"

"It isn't called the high holy holiday for nothing," I replied.

"I just don't understand why the drag queens need to come."

"Pardon me?"

"I mean, its about men and sex and sweat and stuff. Not about drag."

"Not about drag, really? All leather is hyper-masculine drag. It's not all that different from the hyper-feminine of the drag queens."

"Leather is not drag. It's an extension of my natural masculinity."

"How is that different than feeling beautiful in a dress? For drag queens it's an extension of their natural femininity. It's their freedom of expression, and even more then leather, it's art. You know, I think I may have just figured out the difference between a drag queen and a leather man."

"What's that?"

"Drag queens aren't threatened by leather guys."

PANDERING

She got on the crowded train. It was standing room, which meant she wouldn't get any laptop time. She sipped her latte, and glanced at Facebook on her phone. At the next stop, a man got off and another man took his seat before she noticed it.

"You know, it's usually polite to offer the seat to the lady first, " said another woman sitting across from him, in a motherly tone.

"Which panders to the outdated stereotype that women are the weaker, lesser sex, therefore can't be asked to stand until their stop. Such a theory I am sure you don't agree with. So by doing as you suggest, I devalue her as a fellow human being by saying, 'You are weaker and less strong than I am; take my seat,' and in all fairness, I have been standing for seven stops, while she just got on," he calmly and methodically replied.

NOBODY WANTS THAT

I let out a small groan as the alarm went off. I reached over and clicked it off. I sat there in the silence for a moment considering the incredibly ridiculous bike ride I'd done the day before.

"You'd better get up or you're going to be late," the husband mumbled in the dark.

"I hurt everywhere," I replied.

"Yep."

Ten more minutes passed and he rolled over and put his hand on my stomach.

"Now you're going to be rushing around like a whirling dervish, and panicking to be out on time. You really ought to get going."

"Oh Mom, do I have to?" I said. "Can't we just call in sick and stay right here all day long?"

"Nope."

"Why not?"

"Because if the dog pees on the carpet because you haven't taken her out, then you'll have to deal with

271

grumpy husband, and let's be honest, nobody wants that."

And with that I was up and out of bed.

FOOTBALL

"Atta boy, girlfriend!" I blurted at the television, watching football.

My football buddy stopped mid-nacho munch and looked at me. Clearing his mouth with some beer, he said, "I'm not sure a 280- pound cornerback would appreciate being called 'girlfriend.'"

"Look, watching football is already a demerit on my fag card. I'm not going totally straight for this."

"Well, you did leave the sparkly pompoms behind this week. I think you are getting straighter each week," he teased.

We returned our attention to the game, when suddenly our team broke free and ran almost the entire length of the field for a score. We both cheered.

Seizing my moment, I grabbed my crotch and grunted, "fucking great game, dude" and pretended to 'tobacco spit' in my soda. Football buddy laughed mid-beer swig, which caused him to spectacularly spit beer out his nose.

"That was unfair!" he protested.

"Oh, butch it up Louise," I said, with a victorious smile.

EQUALITY

A few DVDs, a pair of earphones and some neatly folded t-shirts and underwear sat there. Every night when I came home, the small box of stuff taunted me, reminding me of all of it.

He had changed his Facebook profile to read "engaged to," so absolutely sure he knew all the answers. He'd posted photos for all our friends to see of the engagement ring.

You always read about fairytale proposals. You daydream of how you might answer when that special moment comes. You imagine yourself at city hall in matching suits.

"What do you mean, what? Seriously? I don't understand?" he said, instantly seething and visibly outraged. "Did the community fight for marriage equality for no reason? We can GET married!"

I figured saying "No, that's not what I want." was enough. We sat in a punishing silence before he simply got up and left my flat.

UNKA

The young girl examined the vegetables. Being shorter, she felt most attached to the carrot on the bottom. She didn't realize she'd bring the whole display down upon her, resulting in a falling cascade of carrots, pelting her.

She was about to erupt in tears when he seemed to appear out of nowhere. He knelt down, whispering comfort in her ear. She hugged him tight, managing a little smile, as he picked the carrots up from around her feet.

"Tank you, Unka," she said in the softest young person speak, still a little ruffled by the situation.

He picked her up and showed her the rest of the vegetable section. He spoke in the calmest gentle voice.

"Mr. Celery and Mr. Bell Pepper, Miss Eggplant. Oh, and Mr. Broccoli. We love Mr. Broccoli, huh? Mr. Basil, Ms. Ginger Root..." He continued with her down the aisle.

In today's world full of people pushing and shoving their way to everything, gentleness can be incredibly difficult. It is always worth it.

BROKEN

"Ya know he went to Vietnam, right?" he said, sipping coffee in the coffeehouse.

"The same Vietnam that ended 40 years ago?" I said, unimpressed.

"That doesn't seem very respectful."

"So, let me get this straight? We're giving him a free pass to be a drunken pathological asshole because he's a veteran? That's weak sauce."

"I'm not saying that at all. I'm saying that at 19, they handed Max a loaded machine gun and said, "kill everything thatta way." He did, and saw things that you and I can't even begin to imagine, and it wrecked him up a little bit. Imagine yourself at 19, out in a jungle full of landmines and bugs and shit everywhere. But you can't. The only sacrifice you make is trying to decide between a peppermint mocha and a caramel macchiatto. Give the girl a break. I'm not telling you she's perfect, but she's broken. And you need to respect that."

BLU-RAY

"Hayden Christiansen!" he screamed, sitting straight up in bed.

"You are such a dorkzilla," said his husband, now also awake.

"What?" I said, blearily.

"You had the 'Hayden Christiansen is the new doctor' nightmare again."

"Damnit, that is twice this week; sorry lovey."

"It's all okay. I knew campy, sci-fi-related nightmares were part of this carnival ride."

"What I don't understand is why *Prometheus* didn't give me nightmares. I mean, the whole thing makes no sense. And I wanted to hand Charlize Theron a Twinkie or some carbs through the whole film. I worry about her; being so thin isn't healthy."

"It's all good, just don't let me catch you with your pants down with *Star Trek Six*'s Christopher Plummer as Chang freeze-framed. That was awkward."

"Wow. You know that was six years ago, right? Before

Thor and before the original *Magnum P.I.* episodes were available on Blu-ray."

"I do, but it's delicious to terrorize you with."

AWKWARD

"I'm sorry," read the magnetic Scrabble pieces on the fridge.

"Well, I'm sure you are," I muttered to myself, sipping morning coffee.

I smiled, actually, at the antics he'd been up to the night before. Nobody is a more adorable drunk than my husband. He gets cuddly and extremely affectionate. He's rather kissy on everyone actually. Which is absolutely fine until I found him at the bar, sharing a kiss with my ex. My ex who shot me that, 'even your husband knows I'm hot' smug mean look. Well, and let's face it, while he is a sociopath and an asshole, he's a furry carpet out of a *Colt* magazine fantasy.

The hubby knew he'd messed up as soon as he saw me. I shot a look at my ex, and politely said, "Come on honey. Let's go home before you need to spend a week at the clinic getting daily penicillin shots."

TRUTH

I realize that Wonder Woman's lasso of truth isn't 'supposed' to be used to coerce people in everyday situations, but think of the possibilities.

Cute guy at the bar tells you he's single. Time to lasso that hot mess up. You find out about his partner, his meth habit, and how he can see you on Tuesdays between 5-9 p.m. and Fridays from 1-5 p.m., and that he considers that a relationship.

Your niece and 2nd grade homework while you babysit: the lasso reveals that story problems piss her off because nobody really goes to the store and thinks how many lemons would I need to buy to equal the weight of the oranges. It's a waste of her time. (That's my girl!)

Take your car to the mechanic, and ask for a quote. You know what to do.... lasso that shit up! Besides, he's a hot ginger muscle bear who looks hot all tied up, so it's a win-win.

HELLO

The waiter escorted him and his date past my table. I smiled, waved and said hello. He walked past me like I wasn't even there.

I headed to the restroom before departing. I was washing my hands when his voice snarled from behind me.

"Pro tip, boy. Waving at tricks in restaurants is totally classless. Now you've got my husband wondering who the fuck you are. Way to fuck up my date night."

I turned to him, drying my hands with a towel. Oh, how I hate being called 'boy' in that kind of dismissive, mean tone.

"I hope you at least had the decency to change the sheets on the bed we fucked in before he got home," I responded. "That a wave from a man in a restaurant can 'ruin date night' is all about you. I feel sorry for your husband."

He stood there, silent and stunned, then growled, "fuck you," and left the restroom.

VIBRATIONS

Arriving early, as always, I was the only patient in the waiting area. The old school receptionist tapped away. Her large Lee press-ons exaggerating the click of data entry. She wore glasses, held to her outfit by a classic 1950s string of white pearls.

The med tech stood next to her, chatting. What I thought at first was an optical illusion soon became a truly visible glow all around the med tech. Then suddenly, with an almost imperceptible snap sound, he evaporated like something out of a sci-fi movie.

I let out a loud, audible gasp, looking to the receptionist.

She stopped, looked over her glasses and said, "Don't mind Vince; we've told him repeatedly that a seven-shot mocha will vibrate him into another dimension. But does he listen, no."

"Just be glad he didn't evaporate during a blood draw," she said, nonchalantly returning to her clicking.

FEAST

The sun crept through the shades and he rolled over for a cuddle. He sniffed slowly along my back and up my neck.

"Oh god yes, nachos with extra cheese and jalapenos. Ooooh and peppermint milkshake, fuck, you smell good," he said, rolling in against my back.

I immediately began regretting my mini-lecture the night before about "we need to eat better, that we are what we eat."

"Oh my little nacho cheese dip," he giggled, sarcastically.

I turned and licked his chin and cackled, "I'm tasting the rainbow…"

Not about to let me win the duel, he grabbed my head and spoke in porn Daddy voice, "Oh yeah, boy, you like that Daddy tastes like meatloaf, don't you boy? You nasty little feeder boy."

I pummeled him with a pillow, laughing, "you still have mashed potatoes and gravy in your beard."

"Then it doesn't count. It's a snack for later…"

FOCUS

The focus group filled out their feedback cards, but we already knew the outcome. The video was our new prototype about protecting yourself from STDs. We'd asked for something fresh, something new and instead we got a narrator sounding frighteningly similar to Marlin Perkins in Mutual of Omaha's *Wild Kingdom*. We hid in the back of the theater hoping nobody would identify us as the makers of this terrible adventure in film making.

Thirty minutes of gut-wrenching failure. The poorly written dialogue elicited involuntary groans and caused one young man to scream out "Boring!" and another to say "Has anyone in this video actually had sex with a man?" Worst was one feedback card that read, bluntly, "Your spokesman needs to see a professional for the mustache dye job. Sure, it's probably fine from across 440 on a crowded Sunday, but in HD widescreen, Just for Men just isn't all that sexy."

STRAIGHT-ACTING

"I don't get this shit," he said, pointing at the personals in the back of the gay newspaper. "Is there a more self-hating term for a fag to use than 'straight-acting'? Talk about a boner killer."

"Pro tip: Sucking cock or getting fucked is hardly something a straight person would do. Kneeling and begging for it isn't incredibly straight either."

"Here we are, years past Stonewall and someone wants to fuck you, but in a 'straight way.' That shit is fucked up."

"Maybe it is somebody's way of saying 'I'm new to gay sex'?"

"Then just SAY that. It's time for gays writing personal ads to use their 'big boy words' and stop with the stupidity."

"Oh, I know. We could teach an online course, 'Personal Ads: Let's get you fucked.'"

"I can see you with the Madonna headset, like a TED Talk."

"It really is all about the accessories, isn't it?"

TOLD

"How come nobody told me that he was a scary, socially-awkward, obsessive stalker?" I protested.

"Because nobody is stupid enough to ask Steve out a SECOND time. You bang that incredible, furry hot body then,' Barnum snarked, continuing, chanting with hand air-quotes for each letter, "R...U...N...A...W...A...Y."

"Is this in some manual somewhere?"

"No, dear. It means that when he mentions how his seafood entree reminds of him of *Dr. Who*, that means you bang that unforgettable furry ass and block his number."

"The whole 'I see Daleks in my pasta' thing didn't seem like a red flag, it seemed, I don't know...adorkable. But, holy crap, how can somebody be so incredibly naughty and delicious, and believe me, he is," I said, fanning myself, "also be such a horrible, frightening hot mess?"

"Welcome to San Francisco, sweetybear. Welcome to San Francisco."

THE EX

Gay-n'-gray would be the shits if it wasn't for friends. Being 50, let's face it, is not for the weak.

He and I dated when we were both 25-year-old baby gays. Who the hell knew what we wanted at 25? I'm nearly 50 for christssake and I don't know!

He always makes time for me. We'll meet for dinner and laugh over wine. I can relax, talk about my problems and he lets me vent.

He's old-fashioned and one of those "OMG let's be like the hetero married gays." We bicker. I love telling him how fucking married guys is the hottest. Complete with crude hand gestures because it gets him so riled up. I use words like 'daddy' and 'rimming' at the table just to see him blush and say, "You know, you're confirming all the reasons you're an ex, right?"

I love him, though. We've made very different lives for ourselves, but I still do.

....

I'll ask him to leave his cell phone in his car, so he won't spend half our dinner together texting or Instagramming his meal. I'll hear all the best hits, including 'Shit, I'm Old,' 'I Get Tired of Being Daddy All the Time,' and 'The Best Sex is With Married Men (I Can Give Them What They Really Want).'

He'll reminisce about the nine months we dated, 24 years ago, like it was yesterday. He'll reach to my plate and take food without asking. He'll patronize the waiter if she's a woman and embarrassingly flirt if he's a man. He'll 'forget' his wallet and ask if I'll get it 'this time.'

"Why do you do this to yourself?" my hubby will say when I get home.

"Because even people I will never understand deserve a little compassion now and then," I'll say, while pouring myself a strong gin and tonic.

THE BET

He came out of the hotel towards the pool. The humidity misters made it seem like something out of a Cirque show.

We watched him as intently as an audience at Wimbledon. He ordered a scotch with seltzer on the rocks. I could hear my hubby start to hyperventilate as he took his shorts off to reveal a Speedo.

"Down boy; you are so not right," I whispered.

"I am so going to win this one," he said confidently.

The man dove in, swam to the side and pulled himself up in front of us, showing his religious preference. At this point, we were both swooning.

"Wait for it; wait. for. it.," I said.

Just then, a blonde with breasts not of this world came out and joined the man poolside, enjoying a rather public lascivious kiss.

"I win. Again," I said with a sly smile.

"This shit is rigged," my hubby said, handing me $5.

THE KEY

"I just want to hit you," he said coldly.

Sitting across the table was his boyfriend, whom he'd broken up with that afternoon.

"You should," said the man across from him.

"I need your key."

"Please…"

"No please, I need your key."

The man got out his keys, unclipped a pair, and set them on the table.

He took the keys in his hands, glared across the table, then got up and left. He was thankful his ex hadn't tried to follow him and continue the conversation.

He walked right past their…his apartment. He wasn't ready to be there. His therapist will look at him with her big Indian eyes and suggest forgiveness, asking him to meditate and not be angry. His friends will not call for a few days, giving him space.

What he wanted more than anything was a boyfriend he could trust again.

FASHION

Despite making the blocked door alarm screech, he held the commuter train door for her.

She was beautiful. She wore red Egyptian cotton with a tweed skirt, flawless makeup, and accessories that showed attention to detail.

"Take a picture, perv, it'll last longer," she said, spitefully interrupting his admiration.

He looked away, thought about it, then turned back to her and spoke, "I held the door for you. I'm not a gentleman for just anyone. I was about to compliment your gorgeous en'semb," he said motioning at her up and down "but since that avalanche of bile came out of your mouth, it makes it hard to imagine having one complimentary thing to say about you. For the record sweetness, no beard, no balls. You're not my type. We. Are. Done."

The train stopped at the next station. Door opening, he abruptly departed.

Someone on the train whispered, "Ooooooh, snap!"

WRITING ABOUT SEX

"This project is really hard," one student offered.

"He said hard. Heh, heh, heh," another responded, in his best Beavis impersonation.

"Thank you, one per class, and frankly, you wasted that one," said the professor, continuing, "Writing about sex is one of the most difficult things you'll ever do."

"Mine reads like IKEA instructions. Bill put part G in Marsha's Part B...and I hate naming all the parts," a student said, to understanding nods.

"Well, try concentrating on how Bill and Marsha feel."

"Bill feels like a man," offered a male student, loudly.

"You're a pig," a woman responded.

"You could both be right. Context is important to give in a sex scene. Maybe Bill is sleeping with Marsha to feel like a man. That gives you context."

"That makes Bill a pig."

"Perhaps so...but at least with context he becomes a well-conceived and believable pig."

TWENTY

"After you pay the $35 reconnection fee, we will have service back on in 48 hours," she said.

"*Game of Thrones* is on tonight; you can't send someone out tonight?"

"No, Sir. Service hours are 8 a.m. to 6 p.m."

"You people are useless."

"Can I interest you in automatic bill pay? That way your payment will happen autom-"

"Charge me the goddamn fee and turn my shit back on."

"Is there anything else I can help you with today, Sir?"

"No. Fuck You, very much."

"Thank you for calling Cable. Have a great day," she said, tapping the 'end' key.

She took her headset off, let out a deep sigh, and took a sip of her Snapple. She took the Sharpie and put a black notch next to 'goddamn' and 'fuck you.'

That was 20 'fuck you's and it was only 10:30 a.m. It was going to be a long day.

SCI-FI

"Why do you watch sci-fi, anyway?" asked my roommate, as he plopped down on the couch. "I mean, I get shit blowing up and the moral dilemmas, but doesn't anyone in outer space fuck?"

"Here we go," I responded, rolling my eyes.

"I mean there is the occasional romantic kiss, but you'd think after being chased across the galaxy by a race of vicious space bad guys, I mean, wouldn't the stress level be less if before, " he said raising his hands in air quotes, "'beaming down' they got down doggy-style? I mean, I always feel better after a fuck. It's like spraying yourself with stress-be-gone."

"...and where are the gays in your precious *Star Wars*? I hope Skywalker's kid is a big flaming ABBA-loving queen. Ooooooooooh, and his nemesis can be Darth Hideous. Only a Sith would wear that shirt with those shoes," he continued.

"You are not well."

OPEN

"Are you listening to yourself?"

"What?!"

"He's cheating on you with another guy!"

"Reel it in, Morticia. Mitch and I have an open relationship, and I actually think Bill is sorta cute."

"Whoa, whoa, whoa, an open relationship? I thought you were all, like, the poster child for monogamy and marriage and stuff."

"And stuff? Mitch gives me no reason to be jealous. We trust one another. And he has always had the ginger boy thing anyways."

"Isn't this a bit like having your cake and eating it too? Isn't one guy enough?"

"I love Mitch; we are always going to be husband…"

"…and wife?"

"Bitch. As I was saying…we are always going to be husbands. But sometimes friendships can be complimented with some intimacy that can sometimes be sexual, or simply super touchy feely."

"I am only bitching because I am jealous, ya know."

"Yeah, I know," he replied, winking. "Ya know, I love ya more than my luggage, the Hello Kitty plastic set. But nonetheless, the love is there."

"Whatever you say, Muriel."

ALWAYS REMEMBERING

Some choices we live not only once but a thousand times over, remembering them for the rest of our lives.

Richard Bach

SWEATER WEATHER

I would ask each Saturday morning of September if it was time yet, even if it was 80 degrees outside. One quiet Saturday morning we'd wake up to the sparkle of the first frost of the season on the grass out front, with the ocean's fog dancing across the surface.

It was like Christmas came early for six year old me. My mother would retrieve the box of sweaters from the attic that we'd carefully folded and put away the spring before. Finally, I was reunited with my favorite pullovers, button ups, vests and my favorite, the cardigans. I would pull out each one and look at it. I'd already preemptively cleared a drawer in the dresser, and refolded each of them carefully and reverently. Forty years later, I still get that rush of romantic energy as the leaves start to gently turn into fall. The return of sweater weather.

REVOLUTION

The thick sweat stuck him to the sheets as he slowly woke up. A horrible night's sleep full of dreams he was actually thankful he couldn't remember. Despite getting almost no rest overnight, his body was sore, telling him he'd been laying there long enough. He got up and walked slowly to the bathroom.

Taking a hand towel and drying himself off, he realized he could hear cars going by on the street outside. He could hear the coffee pot sputtering away in the kitchen. Somewhere outside a dumpster lid slammed up and then back down on the pavement at the untender mercies of a predawn garbage truck. He could hear neighbor kids heading for the elementary school down the block. It was as if when he was asleep the world hadn't been revolving, his few steps pushing it all into forward motion once again.

NO DROUGHT

The hot shower poured over me. I just sat there. Fuck the drought. The grandfather clock in the hallway struck three a.m.; nobody would know I was wasting water anyhow. I reached for the giant glass of pinot noir and took a big deep sip.

I smelled my hands, the last remnants of the smoke from his short wooden pipe on the bar patio danced to my senses. I had been out in the sun sweating in my leathers all afternoon. You could almost feel the water breaking up the sunscreen, smokiness and sweat, breaking them apart into individual elements to stream down my body. I scratched my hair and beard.

We'd made out for two hours in the corner of the bar between occasional mouthfuls of beer we'd shared. He had that thick accent, and honestly just a few words of English at his disposal. The smile that refused to leave my face let me know that was more than enough.

A NEW HOST

He pulled the box down from the top of the closet and reverently set it on the bed. Opening it was like opening a time capsule.

The thin leather vest, the harness both got set aside in the 'will never be that thin again' pile. He smiled, picking up the red lycra tank top, flooding him with memories. God he'd been a hot fucker in that shirt, he could remember dancing at the warehouse till morning. He briefly sniffed the shirt before adding it to the pile.

He folded Richard's chaps neatly. How was it 25 years already?

He'd written in the card, " An eon ago I wore these at the Lure the spring your parents met. Now that I'm a dinosaur, figured I'd pass these onto you. Such an amazing time to be queer don't you think? Love, Uncle Jack."

He stood in line later at the UPS store, holding the package to his chest. He tried to imagine his sisters son opening the box. He knew that leathers mean different things for people. He wondered to himself about the adventures they'd be on with a new host.

THE ROYAL DONUT SHOP

The Royal Donut had been a neighborhood destination for decades. The smell of freshly slathered ring donuts hit you as you turned the block. The atmosphere was charged by the childhood memories the smell created. You could almost watch new customers be struck by, and then get lost in, the wave of nostalgia.

Oscar was behind the counter, a muscular man in his mid-thirties. Locals remembered him starting there as a bright-eyed teenager. He ran around like a whirling dervish refilling coffees and learning early to casually, but purposefully, up sell a prepackaged dozen donut holes.

When his father died suddenly the previous spring, it was assumed the business would disappear. Surely, we thought, such a prime location would become another trendy Euro cafe with designer lattes and overpriced store-bought coffee cake. Oscar simply showed up behind the counter a week or so later, as if he had always been there.

I wondered if Oscar had returned out of a sense of duty. Off in some other life, only to be called up to take over the Royal. I imagined him giving notice at his job, and with solid conviction, returning to the shop on Main Street.

The torch passed, the old ladies would gossip over how long Oscar would remain single. Kids would wink and charm their way to a kid-sized bagel.

He was very sure to use all of his father's old-fashioned terms and phrases.

"Krullers are fresh; maple bars are fine too."

"Fresh cuppa?"

"How about a bag of donut holes with that?"

RED HANKY

The bar manager approached me apprehensively as I was setting up the sound equipment. Thursday nights the bar hosted 'Beareaoke' for the local bear club to come and drink beers and sing.

"We have a problem, Bill," he said. "Rex at the bar double-booked Beareaoke with Red Hanky Social Night. What will we do?"

"Me and Gladys," I said, referring to the drag queen I co-hosted with, "are showmen; we'll figure it out."

Gladys showed up perfectly dressed in a bright red sequin dress. She and I talked about the situation, and decided on the perfect solution.

The bar started filling with a mix of bears and the expected guys flagging red left and right. It was show time, and Gladys stepped up to the microphone.

"Welcome to Beareoke Night at The Dive. Tonight is special. Rex, our hunky bartender, invited the red hanky club along to share this festive evening. So, in honor of that, we will be replacing the word 'love' with 'glove' in any song you sing this evening."

I started the machine and Gladys started her opening number. The familiar tunes of a familiar Elvis song began. Guys and gals looked at each other a bit confused; Gladys didn't usually sing Elvis.

"Take my hand," she began, "take my whole arm too. Cuz I can't help putting my glove in you."

The bar went absolutely ballistic with laughter, and the night was off and running. Highlights of the evening's performances included "All You Need is Glove" by the Beatles, "Endless Glove" from Diana Ross and Lionel Ritchie, "I'm All Out of Glove" by Air Supply, a show stopping "How Deep is Your Glove" from the BeeGees, finally ending at 2 a.m. with a drunken, lighters out, swaying, stirring rendition of "Seasons of Glove" from *Rent*.

REBECCA

He imagined a brilliantly set holiday dinner table. It has been cleared, but for maybe a missed gold fork or knife. The incredible, perfect meal over, the port is being poured in another room. Someone comes in by themselves and surveys the dining room. They lean in and quietly, almost reverently, blow out the hot flame of the candles, its scent and presence remaining in the room. Small wisps of a particular smoke curling and finding their way to your senses.

That is the way he'd always felt about his passing. For months afterwards he'd dream about conversations. He could never remember them when he woke up, but he knew he'd had them. After he first left, it felt like his voice was still lingering everywhere. A whisper guiding him and an approving nod in his mind when he'd finally found his footing.

He'd called him Becky after the naive Pollyanna in *Rebecca of Sunnybrook Farm*. "Dearest Becky," or in a voice of deep disappointment, "Oh Becky...." His passing had been quick, unlike some of the others of those days. Or at least that's how he chose to remember it. He smiled. Strange the things you choose to romanticize. The anniversary had come and gone again that spring.

It had been a while since he'd heard his voice. Nowadays it was when he'd do something he'd have been particularly proud of or some new adventure that would have surprised him. He could see the smile on his face. "Well," he would have said pausing with that thick southern drawl, "…..just look at you, Becky. You go get' em now."

"NORMAL"

He couldn't remember a time when he felt normal. He woke in the dark to the dim buzz of talk radio and walked to the bathroom. He looked at his face in the mirror, noticing more gray and a few more laugh lines around his eyes. If only he'd laugh less, he giggled to himself.

He was returning to work today. This was a big step, according to his therapist. He hoped they were ready for how this had changed him. His bullshit tolerance was going to be much lower.

The hair had grown back this dense, dirty dishwater color he'd named 'Meh.'

"What color is your hair?" they'd ask.

"It's 'Meh.' I thought of going with 'cat vomit' but when I saw the color 'Meh,' it spoke to me," he'd reply, running his fingers through his hair, glamorously. "Don't you love it?"

His favorite joke, about leaning to the right when he walks because his ballast was off, was one of those jokes that made people think about his cancer. He'd lost a testicle and the lymph nodes in his left groin. When his joke made people confront his reality, they either nervously laughed or said 'Oh, I'm sorry' or some other derivative.

People didn't understand or didn't always appreciate his post-cancer sense of humor. For now, he wasn't too worried about making people comfortable.

LAW AND ORDER

I stood naked in the living room, my cock as hard as steel.
He looked up at me with this puzzled look on his face and
said, "Oh honey, you know tonight is a new episode of
SVU." That is when I realized we were over, a TV series
about violent sexual offenders was more important.

When I moved out on my own, I was struck by how quiet
dinners could be without the dull roar of Rachel Maddow
in the background. A morning cup of coffee did not need
to be shared with an incredibly annoying weather and
traffic bimbo on Channel Eight. In all fairness to my ex, I
never really stood up to the television and how it drove us
apart. The stereotypical silences of a couple in trouble
were filled with commercial breaks and *American Idol*.
Relationships take work to keep things fresh and
fulfilling.

I laugh these many years later. When I head into a difficult
meeting at work, or bring something up with my husband
like taking out the garbage or whether or not I can have
the car today, my mind plays that damn chime from *Law
and Order*. (Duh. Duuh.) The narrator in my head says
dramatically, "In the world of relationship dynamics,
there are guys who love guys. They are called
'homosexuals'; these are their stories. (Duh. Duuh.)"

A MATTER OF PERSPECTIVE

It was a rainy night in the neighborhood, when I saw him through a restaurant window.

He didn't even know I was there. I stopped for a moment, staying off at a distance like a ghost.

Here we were, 22 years later. His beard still a soft black. He still worked out. His ear still twinkled with his taste for sparkling earrings. He still had impeccable taste in clothes. I wondered if he still made fantastic omelets and strong thick coffee on Saturdays. He was with a stocky bear-type guy and a straight couple. He poured wine, and broke out mid-pour in his hearty Russian laugh. The sound seemed to chase away the raindrops and surround me.

I'd told him so many years before, after dating for a few months, that I wasn't ready for a relationship. That I was still so new to being out, that I had more exploring to do. I pulled my coat up around my shoulders and walked away into the dark, ashamed that all Dmitri would remember me for was breaking his heart.

SMELLED LIKE US

What was I doing? He'd broken every conceivable kind of trust, yet here I was, walking home from his apartment. Why was I still sleeping with him, goddamnit? I hated showering at his place; totally gross. Worse, I still smelled like 'us.' I remember when 'us' meant something other than a 10 p.m. call that he was lonely. I hated that sleeping in next to him felt so good. I hated that despite all the horrible things he had done to me that we could collapse in a sweaty pile and sleep together like our bodies were puzzle pieces. He used the word 'baby' as a seductive weapon. His smell, his kiss rendered me helpless. I would have to quit him cold turkey. I would wash 'us' out of my clothes and off my skin and block his phone number, his chat handle, his email. I laughed, imagining my bumbling, clueless ex-boyfriend on the street below my apartment like Stanley Kowalski.

AS MUCH ANYMORE

He awoke there, the glass miraculously still between his fingers, bathed in the springtime full moon's light coming through the slider. He stared down, twirling the glass of wine in his hand dangling lazily. He aimed the remote and turned on the stereo, arpeggios in a minor key. Half a glass of cheap red and he was out like a light. He chuckled to himself, the drinking marathon days of his twenties were surely gone. A lifetime ago, when he'd stumbled out of a bar with him and first brought him home.

It was moments like these, where he would have come home and found him asleep with a book on his chest. They would have talked in the dimly lit room about the book he was reading. Finally, he'd interrupt wherever they were and suggest that they should head to bed. They'd get under the covers, and he'd pretend not to notice that he'd used too much fabric softener, and the bed smelled like a lilac factory. He'd get the giggles and wake up the next morning with beard burn on the scruff of his neck.

He missed him. Thinking about him didn't hurt as much anymore. Remembering reminded him that the past was real. He still kept a box of graham crackers in the pantry because they were his favorite.

STORMS

I grew up on these islands. Soggy, wet and cold winters there, often joking that if I stood still that moss would grow on the north side of my body.

Storms arrived there ferociously. Flanked on the left by the looming Olympic mountains, the sky would turn the darkest grey, the very definition of a tempest. The wind came first, pressing back the evergreens into submission. Out on the beach, some of them had naturally grown like blown back angels, accepting their fate at the will of the wind. The wind would deliver the first raindrops to your face like a stinging bumblebee.

You could stare out over the Salish Sea and see the rest of the storm making slow progress towards you. The deluge would soon surround you, and as a veteran of such days on the islands, you would aim your face up into the rain, then shake your beard free of the raindrops, tighten your hood and continue on your hike along the beach.

GET A HUG

He had this incredibly gentle way of navigating the world. In retrospect, it is not surprising he was the first gay man I fell in love with. I was at a church social and I spied him speaking to someone across the loud, chaotic room in ASL.

It's just about the rudest thing you can do to a deaf person in that situation, stare like a teenage girl getting a peek at Bobby Darin. It was the first time I got a glimpse of that silent snarl of disapproval.

I quickly moved on in the party, and figured I'd totally blown it with him. Not that I've ever had much, but particularly when I was first out of the closet, I lacked any subtlety. I'd like to think over the years I've turned that into a charming trait people appreciate.

I drove up to Washington DC the next weekend; it was the showing of the AIDS Quilt on the Mall. Truly, it was one of the single most impactful experiences of my young gay life. Frankly, it overwhelmed me. So that evening I found myself, as I'm sure others did, up against the wall of the Eagle with a scotch and soda in my hand, trying to shake it off. I looked around the bar. It was a humid evening, and I was appreciating all the barely dressed men parading by. That's when I noticed him again, two hours from our home in Norfolk, across the patio from me. Except, this time it was him that was doing the stare down.

His presence was completely different from the night at the party in the freshly ironed dress shirt. He was beautiful. Short and muscular, and that almost unworldly dark brown beard with a hint of red. Twenty-five-years later and I can still remember every detail. He wore a very tight leather harness, chaps with an old-fashioned, well-worn codpiece. Everything about his outfit showed attention to detail as well as leather that got worn a lot, comfortable leather.

He was smoking a small black English pipe. While we played the stare game, wafts of soft white smoke would leave his lips, hesitating in his whiskers before floating away.

He suddenly signed at me, flashing a pleasing smile. It took me a moment to realize what he was saying, and he repeated himself.

"Come here. Come here and get a hug."

LIKE A CLOAK

We met on a springtime Vancouver afternoon. One of
those days on English Bay where the sky is fresh and the
wind is full. He was flying a kite on the beach and just
shined me this amazing smile. We were soon dating,
attached to each other like Velcro. We spent mad
mornings making love in the shower, and finding places
for hikes in the mountains. We spent a few magical days
sunning at the nude beach and being a happy pair.

It was soon apparent, however, that his smile was rare. He
was overcome and lived in a place of sadness. He'd been
wrecked up by the 80s and 90s being in the middle of the
AIDS epidemic as a nurse. He'd lost the ability to
disconnect himself from everyone he was watching lose,
and had somewhere lost himself. He would go days
where he wouldn't speak and would withdraw. He was
the first true pessimist I'd ever met. He was capable of
quickly identifying the ways an activity could hurt him, or
others, and flat out refuse to experience it based on that
split second decision and judgment. By Labor Day, it felt
like I was the only one initiating anything. I never felt like
he called up and said "Let's go on an adventure" or "I
found this great new restaurant." It was then I realized
he'd put me on the list of the things he was resisting

experiencing, scared of being hurt, scared of the risk that deeper relationships require.

He sent me my key in the mail without even a note. Saying goodbye to him proved to be one of the hardest thing I'd ever done. I have to admit that part of it is that I am a Pollyanna. I am constantly seeking the good things that will happen and actively search for something good in everything. Despite my best efforts, all he wanted to show me was dread and struggle. I'll always remember the smell of him on my sheets after a lurid night of sweaty sex. I'll always remember his smile, and his French Canadian-accented nicknames for me. Not to sound like a self- help book cliché, but in order to be happy about our relationship, I needed to let it go.

Friends asked me why I waited so long, and how could I have not seen what a depressed Debbie Downer he was for me? Love and romance clouds so many things. Where others saw isolation, I saw introspection. Where others saw rudeness, I saw social awkwardness. I wanted it so badly. But even through my polished veneer of positivity, I finally saw that we shouldn't be a couple.

For a while, wherever I'll go I'll wonder where I am in relationship to him. I'll worry if he'll be alone. I'll worry, because that is the compassionate man I am. I am incapable of not caring.

It's a solid truth, that some people have a hard time letting go of their suffering. They wear it like a cloak. Out of self preservation, they prefer the suffering they know versus perhaps letting something new in.

ALBUM

The first time I heard Billy Joel's 'Scenes from an Italian Restaurant' I was ten. Everyone else was humming 'Just the Way You Are' or rebelling by playing 'I'm Movin' Out.' I would listen to 'Italian Restaurant' over and over. The cassette tape was probably extra stressed out from the screeching stop and rewind. I had it timed in my head how to rewind the tape exactly seven minutes and thirty seven seconds. I guess for a precocious ten year old, it felt like listening to an adult version of *Lady and the Tramp*. How you could meet for dinner with someone at 'our Italian restaurant.'

I analyzed lyrics, obsessively writing them all out in my spiral notebook journal, along with cartoon Billy Joel faces in the margins. The poor story of Brenda and Eddie. I had so many childhood friends whose parents were divorced. I remember writing stories, while chewing on #2 pencils, about how Brenda and Eddie found each other again and had a storybook ending. 'A bottle of red, a bottle of white. Whatever kind of mood you're in tonight.'

CRISIS

He'd left the crowded national park's parking lot, and he'd hiked determinedly up and away from them to reach the magic. He couldn't hear car horns, he couldn't hear people talking loudly on cell phones. It literally felt like magic. It was a thick wool comforter he could pull over his mind. Every year it took longer to get outside the wall of sounds and chirp of distractions.

Our present environmental crisis is, in essence, a spiritual crisis. A plague, the revolution that vaulted Christianity to victory over paganism. He could see it's scar in the brown trees striping up the mountainside in front of him.

Inhibitions to the exploitation of nature vanished as the church took the spirits out of the trees, mountains, and seas, placing them instead in steeples and in the grandest of ideology into man himself. The ghost-busting theology made it possible for man to exploit nature in a mood of indifference to the feelings of natural objects. It made nature man's monopoly. That someone could look up this mountainside and see something consumable, a naked resource to be turned into power?

He came here every year, to the sanctuary, to walk among his peers and ask for salvation.

IN THE MIRROR

When he described where he'd been and how he'd lived, how long he'd allowed it to be 'okay,' he realized how many excuses he'd made to endure the situation. How many things he'd allowed to be okay, when just below the surface he knew they were not for a long time.

Petty fear had kept him there. Fear of all the insecurities he'd been trained to accept were true. Fear that if he moved elsewhere, he'd fail. He had learned to forgive those voices that told him that seeking something different was wrong. He still struggled with how much it hurt them for him to leave and never return.

He thinks about it every morning when he steps out of bed onto the ground that is here, not there. However, every step taken in this bright city is nothing like his previous life. He journals about what his parallel life might have been had he stayed. His parents would have been so proud, and he would have found new levels of despair. It had to be left behind on that sudden blustery February afternoon. He can still see the rolling hills disappearing in the rear view mirror. He could remember pulling over to the side of the road, stopping to touch the reflection one last time.

WINDMILLS

One of the most rewarding things about moving into my fifties is that my Don Quixote days are behind me. The Spanish fictional character had been a model for the way I'd navigated a lot of my early life. He was famous for "tilting at windmills," for preparing to do battle with imaginary enemies and for always seeing danger instead of beauty. That was the stopping point for me, when I realized how much beauty I was missing out on tilting against everything in my path.

I could conveniently refer to it as a 'spiritual path' or a 'reconciliation' or some other feel good term, but the truth of the matter is my anger chased a lot of beauty out of my path that will never return. So now when I get an opportunity to bring it close and embrace it, I don't hesitate. There is so much out there that makes you want to stand in a tree like E.M. Forster's George in *Room with a View* and shout "BEAUTY!" All it takes is a calm breath and learning patience to let the world show you all it has. It takes stopping occasionally and letting the beauty reveal itself instead of angrily shouting "WHERE ARE YOU?" because like all things, beauty will hide if you try and shout it out of its hiding places.

A SYMPHONY

He stepped out in the box seat in the symphony hall. He'd been sitting at his desk at work earlier when a pink envelope arrived for him. Inside, scribbled in his impossibly bad handwriting was 'you, me and Arvo, baby! Wear a tie.' He could see the stage set up with a large reed harp at the center. The concierge arrived with a chilled bucket with a bottle of champagne.

The musicians started filing out and getting ready for the performance. The violinists and cellists started playing riffs and warming up. He remained standing, straightening his bright red bow tie. The basses moved in. He loved the bass players, well, his bass player, in particular.

He remembered making out with him in the back of a seedy bar. Of course the biggest, strongest bull of a nasty biker in the bar played in the symphony. Lost in thought and memories, he noticed the small gray box on the seat. Inside were a pair of old-fashioned opera glasses.

As the maestro and choirs came on stage, he futzed with the glasses, scanning down across the orchestra to find his husband's ironman Spanish stare looking back up at him in the box from the back row. Dressed in his tux, the black of his mustache looked even darker than normal. His bass player exchanged some small talk with his stand mate, then managed one last wink and stare up at the box seat.

"Woof," he said under his breath, continuing to look on. His linebacker then got to work, stepping in behind his instrument as the orchestra tuned up one final time. Maestro raised his baton and the program began.

LIPSYNC

He set the bag of groceries down on the counter. Tapping the remote on the stereo, the kitchen filled with the familiar opening bars of "Everything She Wants" by Wham! From the first high pitched "ooh-ah-ooooo," he began lip synching and dancing around the kitchen as he put groceries away. He slid around on the kitchen floor like Tom Cruise. "Somebody tell me, why I work so hard for you?" he sang into the salad dressing bottle. He gleefully broke into ridiculous, silly freezes during the bridge.

He'd owned a white "CHOOSE LIFE!" t-shirt back when the song had originally gone big. He continued dicing avocado and getting salads out as it moved onto the next song.

He felt him move in behind him as he dotted the plates with croutons. Reaching around him and grabbing him by the belt buckle, the chef let out a little giggle as his partner's beard tickled his neck.

They danced around the kitchen island to the disco number in a two-step like a pair of velcro cowboys. He'd push back and they'd arch and get closer and closer, to finally a twirl and a finish and back into a cuddle over not quite finished salads.

His dance partner leaned in, kissing his ear and whispered "Happy Friday, Munchkin."

CULTURE CLUB

The Warehouse was the kind of leather bar where you hummed Culture Club's 'Do You Really Want to Hurt Me' at your own risk. It was something out of a well-used Tom of Finland book as opposed to a shiny, glossy porno. There was something intuitively rougher, experienced and darker about the place. If you wanted to wear leather but not use it, you went to Cuffs or some other S&M (Stand and Model) bar. This was where you went to meet people that had leather that was well worn, experienced and smelled of regular use.

It is gone now, the Warehouse, replaced by overpriced condos and a designer clothing outlet. When I walk by I still smile and remember pipe smoke lingering in my leather vest, the honest smell of a man, ice-cold beer and the large cast of lifetime friendships made in the moody dark of my first leather bar. The evenings there, when I first came out, shaped who I am, and to a great extent, who I will be as a mentor for the new man that sheepishly walks into the new bar down the street on a humid late Saturday night.

F.M.P.

We stacked the cell phones in the middle of the table. No checking your Instagram feed instead of interacting with your friends at the dinner table. First rule of dinner club? That shit can wait.

Drinks were soon delivered and we all got caught up. It was like watching a John Hughes film about fifty-year old homosexuals.

Izze and Bill were off on some new crazy travel adventure involving a hotel made of ice. Michael was still single and still bitter about it, and still keeping his standards for who he wants a relationship with ridiculously high. Rob went on and on, and still more on, about a technical project he was working on and why the javasomethingorother didn't work and how he had to redo it all and save the day. Marc doesn't do a whole lot of talking but is one of the most amazing active listeners I know. He always weirds out the husband asking about a single sentence out of a two-hour conversation, and how he'd like to know more about that single topic amongst the bazillion that get flown over the table during a dinner. Phillip is thankful to have a night off from theater, and always has entertaining "you wouldn't believe what a bitch (fill in the blank with the latest touring female singer) statement. Phillip is 52, but sings backup for young acts because he looks like he's 30. We all hate him, but he comes to dinner anyway. I'm convinced he's like Dorian Gray and one day all the traveling and crazy life he leads will age him in one 35-minute trolley ride to the Symphony Hall. I update people on my writing and how for the 5th year in a row I'm crazy busy writing my new novel. The more champagne that flows, the more adorably drunk my husband gets, and we pour him into the car and head home.

"Boy, those girls have such dramatic lives," he says a bit slurred. "It's so good that you and I are so (burp) issue-free."

"Fucking Mary Poppins, baby, F.M.P; practically perfect in every way," I respond, giggling.

"In bed," he blurts out, finishing my sentence, giggling like a four- year old who just said the word 'penis' for the first time

FLANNEL NIGHTSHIRT

I remember being a small child dressed in a suit designed for adults. She'd promised me she'd be here for Christmas but left us on the 12th.

Forty years later, the handwritten, 'For Richard, from Mum' I'd received from her that year are framed and hanging in my study. Around the room, hung in their own little intimate settings, the individual ornaments Pop had taken us to get each year, our own special way of remembering her.

I could tell you where I was in life when each of them arrived. A Teddy Bear in a masculine red scarf with authentic wire frame Roosevelt glasses when I was studying philosophy at seminary. A beautiful green Jekyll sparkled in the corner for the year I met Michael, and I put my collar away in the dresser. A perfect, round, gold and red ornament behind glass case on a velvet pillow, like Cinderella's slipper, for the year we adopted Mia. Standing tall next to me on my desk, a high-polish toy soldier nutcracker, to remember Pop. Five gold rings on a necklace that Michael had given me when we'd finally been able to get married.

We'd hung this year's tribute on a thick lush red ribbon. A

large intricate crystal snowflake in the center of the picture window. Michael popped his head in around the door frame, his smile lighting up his white mustache. Mia and the kids were pulling up. I set down my book, touching the remote to fill the house with music. I looked back and admired the snowflake-refracted curls of light across the wall.

Late at night we'd wrap presents on the kitchen island. We'd break out the port. While everyone worked on the perfect wrapping, I'd break out the tag set. Alone I would write to each of them in an art school charcoal, 'To Lizzy from Gramps and Granpa', 'To Mikey, from Gramps and Granpa', 'To my darling Mia, and that man she married, from Pop', 'To my Michael, from Gramps.'

I'd toddle off to bed in my flannel nightshirt, muddled by the wine, and very much my mother's child.

I AGREE

I thought at first it was narcissism, that nobody could be that completely clueless about how their actions and decisions affect other people. I realized later than it wasn't just commitment to me he'd had a problem with, but a commitment to anything. But then I started meeting the other people in the "Oh, you dated Jim; oooooh, sorry about that" support group, or OYDJOSAT for short. I came to realize that his entire life is controlled by the next shiny new thing. It's like witnessing ADD on crystal meth. He's so eager to avoid responsibility, he's like a shiny pinball that is constantly ricocheting off of targets with no hope of every really stopping.

That shiny new thing can be a boyfriend, a trick, a career (he's on number six), a house, or as the OYDJOSAT like to call it, his membership to the 'Fetish of the Month' club. I like to imagine as a member of the Fetish of the Month club, Jim excitedly receiving a box of props, a form-fitting outfit du jour, talking points about why it's the best kinky subculture ever, and how it's helping him evolve spiritually, and curiously, points on how all the others were wrong for him and are beneath him now. That way, he can walk into a new room of "fetish soul brothers" each month, shiny and new.

He used that horrible Oprah Winfrey's Book-of-the-Month club cliché when breaking up with me about how "it wasn't me, it was him." It angered and confused the fuck out of me at the time. But now that I'm with a stable, non-pathological, kinky, romantic man that doesn't reboot randomly and is actually aware of his place in my life, I'm actually inclined to agree with him.

DO YOU SNORE?

In the dark, I tried to move the dog who had chosen a position up against the husband's, blocking me from getting any kind of snuggleage. The dog let out this deep whiny growl, letting me know that she was moving by protest. I gently scooted her across the bed down into the fold of my husband's knees. I got back up into bed, pulling the covers up. I snuggled in against him, found the perfect arm angle so I wouldn't wake up later with my left arm asleep and tingly. The dog and I had found the perfect family cuddle configuration. I fell triumphantly asleep only to be wide awake again soon. Between the dog and the husband, the snoring was simply too much. Surrendering, I got up, grabbed a comforter from the hall closet and moved my sleep operation to the guest room. I smiled still being able to hear the snore-a-thon competitors going for gold.

WARMTH

"Holy crap, he's pretty," he thought to himself, looking at the man next to him sleeping. He smiled about how completely drunk they'd both been the night before. How despite all intentions, they'd made out for a while then both fell asleep. It had been a while since he'd had a warm fuzzy back to curl in next to. He had to admit it felt nice to have him here. This was far better than clicking through online profiles hoping he could get the guts to invite someone over. They'd both joined the conversation at the bar on a Thursday, laughing over too many drinks. As he'd reached for his coat, his guest had whispered in his ear how nice it would be to come home and sleep with him. Now, in the early light of the morning, tracing his hand over the strong shoulders next to him in bed, he couldn't help but agree.

FRAME

It had been a good day at the antique stores, particularly the breadbox radio he'd found. There was something appreciatively old world about spending the dark of winter gently sanding and refinishing things, giving them new life. The radio was going to be work, but he loved them the most of all.

He slid the plyboard casing off the back and noticed that taped to the inside was a crusty black and white photo. He guessed by the chrome and fins on the car the man was leaning against, it was somewhere in the mid 1950s. The man in the photo stared into the camera with startling intimacy and affection. He was wearing dirty overalls, perhaps a mechanic? Carefully tapping it free of the tape with a knife, he looked at it up close. Turning it over, inscribed in perfect red ink cursive was, "I will miss you, Michael – Love, Your John."

TEDDY

He struck a match, lighting the lantern. Already in his nightshirt, he walked up the steps to the bed, viewing the valley through the small loft window. The moonlight gave everything almost an active sparkle. The dog was already in his position at the foot of the bed, snoring away.

He grabbed the leather volume and opened it at the red ribbon bookmark. He'd ordered it from a bookseller; he liked leather bound books. They just felt more significant in your hands. He started in, trying to reset his mind to the text.

Roosevelt's speeches, now there was a topic he'd never thought he'd be reading. He was more likely to read about kayak building or some other crazy year-long task involving wood dust and solitude.

"...The credit belongs to the man who is actually in the arena, whose face is marred by dust and sweat and blood..."

He imagined the stocky mustachioed statesman speaking before the crowd in Paris in 1910. He wondered if he knew then how his words would reach into the future.

USS LAPON (1985 to 1989)

He sat in the mess decks aboard ship. They'd finished his formal captain's mast a few minutes earlier, and the corpsman was getting ready to escort him off the boat for the last time.

Alongside a bunch of other reasons, he'd been suspected of homosexuality and was being discharged. The submarine crew had been buzzing with rumors for weeks after someone had anonymously tipped off that he'd been seen coming out of gay bars in Norfolk and frequented gay-owned restaurants and art galleries. He stared down at the manila folder that was the entirety of his military career, wondering what was next, when a voice snarled at him.

"So, McDiarmid, are you a fudge-packer or what?" said the gruff, angry voice.

He looked up across the room at the machinist Neff. Neff was a gigantic man, nearly 300 pounds of muscle and animus.

Before thinking, he replied with a wry dagger of a smile, "Why, Neff? Interested in sucking my cock?"

The speed and agility that Neff exploded across the room

at him was amazing. Neff grabbed him by the collar, McDiarmid staring him down defiantly. The corpsman and the XO stepped into the room. Neff looked up, and roughly released him back into the chair.

"I think it's time to go, McDiarmid," said the corpsman.

"You can step back, Mr. Neff," said the XO.

Neff let out a defeated huff and left the mess decks. The XO and the corpsman escorted McDiarmid up the ladder, past the radio room where he'd worked the last three years, into the control room where he was asked to sign out in the log one last time.

"Can't even stay out of trouble waiting to be escorted off the boat, can you McDiarmid?" said a clearly beleaguered XO.

"I suppose that's why I'm being escorted off the boat, Sir," he said somewhat respectively.

They climbed up the ladder to the top deck, and they escorted McDiarmid to the end of the pier.

"Good luck," said the corpsman shaking his hand. The van was waiting to take him to the processing barracks. A few days later, he'd get in his car and drive out of the gate, no longer a U.S. sailor.

HATE

He gently rubbed his hair back in the steam of the bath. He gazed over at the empty wine glass. He chuckled to himself, "What a sad thing, an empty wine glass is."

He'd thought perhaps he could shake it off but here in the tub, his thoughts got worse. But it was no use, and this year, it was worse than ever. He absolutely hated Christmas.

He had entered the dreaded Christmas media blackout period. Television had been intolerable for weeks already. Commercial radio had become the annual tsunami of commercials singing 'Jingle Bells' set to the words "Shop Shop Shop, Shop Shop Shop." Even the classical music station had switched to all Christmas music, so it was of no use.

He was sure that eventually someone around him would inadvertently "Ho Ho Ho" their way to learning the erotic joy of a bell-shaped butt plug. He only had to make it 14 more days and it would be over. At least until next September 1st.

THE TOILET

We all called it the Toilet. It was the last bar on the row. It was where you might try that last desperate attempt, where you'd get 'flushed' to, the last chance to get laid on your way back to your apartment. You'd walk in, buy a cheap $2 beer, and run to the restroom. You'd take a long look in the mirror, trying to convince yourself that a hopeful, fresh beer at 1:58 a.m. is not desperate.

You'd come out and scan the room, filtering to the lowest common denominators. A sip or two of beer and you'd decide if you were just better off going home alone. Finding someone to keep you warmer the only way a man's body can, someone that could Velcro snuggle up against you. Who here would, in his sleep, pull his arm around you, purring contentedly and snuggle back against your entire body?

BASKETBALL TORTURE HOUR

Returning to school in the fall only meant one thing, the return of Basketball Torture Hour (BBTH). It rotated through my junior high schedule like a specter.

First off, let's just say yellow and red are not good colors on me. I was already the runt. I didn't need any help from the school colors of my gym uniform, which made me look like I was on death's doorstep.

Everything from dribbling the ball across the court to practicing trying to shoot a basket was an exercise in futility. By the time actually playing games came around, I'd made it abundantly clear to my classmates that I was not meant for the sport. Someone would pass me the ball, and I'd panic, the ball hitting my chest or my face, my opponent scooping up the ball and stealing it away.

I have no idea what the planned lesson was supposed to be for BBTH, but for me at the time, it was perseverance.

BELLS

He'd imagine proud parents dropping kids off on a sparkling autumn morning. He would put on the special blue-gray cardigan sweater he was known for, tightening his bow tie, putting on his game face, and welcoming a new room full of explorers. His walls would be plastered with turkeys made from handprints and 'the word of the day.' He would look forward to the younger sisters of former students, and guard himself against six-year-olds who already knew that 'cute' could get them whatever they wanted.

This fall was different, though. He smiled as he flung the pack over his shoulder. He'd been thinking of this particular day for five, maybe even ten years. This September third, as the bells rang in the new year at Addison Elementary, he was hundreds of miles away grabbing his walking stick and hiking into the first fall sunrise of retirement.

HOPELESS PLACE

I pulled over to the side of the road, wiping tears from my eyes. "Goddamnit," I said to myself, "it's only a fucking Rhianna song; pull it together Mary." Only I'd heard it differently that morning.

I was in my car dancing along to the open bars, "We found love in a hopeless place," she sang, "It's the way I'm feeling I just can't deny, but I've gotta let it go."

He has been gone now 20 years. He was already poz and quite sick when we met. When he realized we were falling in love, he held me in the dark of a rainy Seattle night. He spoke and I could feel tears on my back. He told me that it was too late for him to be loved. To love him was hopeless. I told him it was simply too late. We made love that night and never spoke about hopelessness again.

BELLINGHAM 1989

He'd found the bar in a hastily grabbed copy of the gay
rag from the adult book store on Holly Street. He'd been
keeping the address scribbled on a matchbook in his
pocket for weeks. How was he expected to find the stuff of
love songs in a dark smokey bar? His life as a gay man
had consisted of driving up to the rest stop on the
interstate. What started as dark nights of fast and furious
discovery, quickly started leaving him wanting more.
How do you say hello? How do you ask a man out on a
date? He ordered a beer. He scanned the faces of the men
around the room. What did he look like, the man he
wanted to hold hands with, the first man he'd spend the
night with. He desperately wanted someone to tell him
that it's all going to be okay.

TIGER

Just the sound of his voice over the telephone lit up my day. With the time difference, he was already well into his morning. It meant he'd had to take a break to give me a call. I tried to keep it fresh and upbeat and not let him hear even a moment of negativity.

We'd dated for nine months. We held hands walking through Alcatraz. We'd jumped out of airplanes tethered to one another. We'd made love in every conceivable part of my flat. We'd found the spiritual in each other.

Then, in an instant, his job moved him back east. He said, "I have to go, Tiger," and the phone clicked.

The Buddha says that "in the end, all that matters is how much you loved, how gently you lived, and how gracefully you let go of things not meant for you." I collapsed against the restaurant window and quietly cried.

STAIRWELL

We met on the old wooden stairs of the old DC Eagle. It had this big dramatic landing between flights of stairs, with enough room for a couple of people to stand and watch the parade. He wore a pair of tight blue jeans, big boots, and a green tank top with the word "DADDY" across the chest. He had that not quite five o'clock shadow thing going on with his beard, but the thickest most amazing mustache I've ever known. I literally stopped in my tracks the first time up the stairs walking past him. Upon my third attempt at passing by, he reached out and grabbed my belt loop, pulling me in against him and over the loud music playing in the bar, growled in my ear, "And just where do you think you're going? You just stay here with me for a little while."

PILLIERS DES BARS

Philip was, as we say, a 'pilliers des bars,' a pillar of the bar. He is always there at 3 p.m. with his Sapphire and soda, smiling and enjoying a cigarette. The hubby calls them the pillierettes. A group of older gay men for whom pre-happy hour cocktails is the homosexual version of a knitting circle.

They gossip, laugh, smoke, talk about the state of the neighborhood, and after a few drinks reminisce about a life before AIDS and before equality, where life was the struggle to not be invisible. They were once the twenty-year-olds bravely marching in 1970 pride marches. They were the thirty-year-olds screaming "ACT UP! FIGHT AIDS!", they were the forty-year- olds looking around and realizing their entire generation seemed to be missing.

They look out on the street now and see equality. They look out on the street and see a glimmer of hope for the end of AIDS. And for all that work, they deserve pilliers status. Salutè.

TACO BELL

There is only one rule for relationship success. It's easy: no Taco Bell. My boyfriend needs to care about his body more than to be caught dead face first in a macho chalupa with green sauce. When a sauce's first ingredient is "green color #12" we are in trouble.

That afternoon when I'm cleaning the car, I find a $1.50 taco wrapper in the glove box. The house smells like cinnamon coffee cake, and classical music is playing when I get upstairs. He knows I've found it.

He's in the kitchen and he gives that powerful pout and says, "I was weak."

"It's okay. I'll just make a tofu scramble for dinner, my little furry chalupa bear." I couldn't keep a straight face smiling as I said it.

"Chalupa bear?" he responded.

"I love romantic nicknames, and that even made ME throw up in my mouth a little."

He got off lucky.

SANDALWOOD

"Etch-eynne I-badoh" was how his French accent pulsated his name out when we met on the ferry to Seattle. I had been out on a hiking camping trip and I smelled something like sandalwood rubbed with wet salmon. I was the dictionary definition of "holy crap, what is that smell?" – yet he flirted with me anyhow. I had two-day beard, was wearing faded flannel and bare feet in sandals. He had a thick black mustache and sturdy strands of body hair pushing through the threads on his t-shirt. He bought me a coffee and a donut, and we swooned on each other the entire crossing. He came over for dinner that night, and while he enthusiastically recommended a shower, he asked me nicely not to shave. I got him fresh tulips. Five years later, I still have to clean the bathroom drain covers daily of his slowly graying flock of hair, and I haven't shaved since.

OVERSHARE

The dinner party erupted in laughter as he finished the story.

"You all know I married a fiction writer, right?" his husband added with fake disdain. "All of his versions of these stories are 'novelizations,' a romantic vision of a much less complicated story."

He kept pouring the wine and champagne. Stories and jokes are always funnier if you keep your guests in that careful zone between not-quite-sober and not-quite-drunk.

Marcia and her partner, who always reminded him of Peppermint Patty and Marcy from *Peanuts*, had a high threshold. They could drink all night and be just fine.

Martin, on the other hand, had to be closely monitored. He looks at a bottle of hard liquor and is soon smacking asses regardless of the sex and telling of his adventures as a fisting bottom at the Sling, with great detail. Yeah, we try to keep that from happening again.

MISSIONARIES

We're out in the yard one day and we see them coming from blocks away. I turn and say, "Here's our chance; get ready!" He disappears into the house as I patiently wait for them to come knocking.

Inviting them in, I call out in a loud voice, "Dad!? Come meet our new friends!"

My husband steps up behind me in head-to-toe leather, leashes and floggers clipped to his hip. He reaches around and pinches my nipples and I respond with a theatrical whimper.

He looks up towards the two missionaries and snarls, "Oh… they'll do nicely, VERY nicely."

Elder Fetner and Elder Marsh take a moment to consider the situation and almost make a Looney Tunes-silhouette exit through the screen door.

I always get a satisfied smile when they return to our block, and upon looking at a neighborhood map, literally cross the street rather then come near our sidewalk.

AFTERWARDS

The car radio blared Oingo Boingo, the smell of the joint still lingered. We rode along quietly, my hand on his hip. The drive back from Pocatello was long and boring. The funeral was beautiful, but it was a tumultuous time for his family to meet me.

His Pop was understandably shaken. They had been out at lawn bowling. She was in his favorite floral skirt and yellow sunhat. The next moment she was gone. He was thankful that she'd not felt a thing.

His mother had been a powerhouse matriarch for 50 years. The shell shocked looks on everyone's faces said they weren't sure how the rest of their lives would go down in her absence. He turned to me as the car sped down the freeway, a tear in his eye, and suggested perhaps everyone would finally be free to be themselves for the first time ever.

SLEEPING BEAUTY

He sat with his head leaning against the glass. White earphone cords lead across his flannel shirt to his pocket.

Eyes shut, he nodded slowly to the music as a contented sleeping smile swept across his face. He held a large leather-bound journal, liberally decorated with Easter-egg colored sticky notes. He was almost cuddling with it like he was under the covers.

He smelled of sandalwood and coffee. He had missed a half-inch spot in that morning's shave. I was feeling guilty at having him all to myself when his phone erupted in vibration.

"Hello…" he said softly.

Nodding in agreement, he listened, then said confidently, "Don't make it complicated, who equals subject, whom equals object, who is he or she, whom is her or him."

"You're welcome," he said, hanging up and curling back up to sleep with his journal.

My sleeping beauty was an English major.

LESSON

I could hear the nurses talking out at the nursing station.

I'd caused an ugly scene yesterday. I didn't want to be on this wing. These are the rooms where others had come and never escaped. Two doors down was the piano player from the sweater bar. Next door, the kind man who loved wearing Liberace-style fur coats and loved sunflowers.

Wasn't there room somewhere else in the hospital, goddammit? Don't put me in a room to die. I was sure I wasn't the first angry, scared person to occupy room #703.

I stared out the hospital window. The clock showing 2 a.m. I glanced over at the untouched birthday cake the boys had brought by earlier. You know I'm sick if I don't want to touch cake. I smiled, looking up at the helium Hello Kitty balloon.

I sat there bathed in moonlight, no longer feeling invincible.

CHATTING

Apparently, I talk too much during sex to go to sex clubs anymore.

I guess I'm old-fashioned. What happened to some high quality intimate pre- and post-orgasmic chatter?

I know we live in the 140-character world now, but has it really just come down to "pay your $12, get in, get off, go home"?

No chatter about how much I hate Ross on *Friends*?

Or how bad that new overpriced restaurant is in the Castro?

Or why stretch pants are NOT pretty and should simply be illegal? Or about how fabulous the latest production at the opera was?

This certainly isn't like *The Ritz*, darlings.

Recently, I was banned from one place for dictating one of my grandma's prize-winning recipes in the darkness of their blow job maze. "People don't come to the suck palace to hear about your meatloaf, buddy. Save that shit for the Eagle's patio beer bust."

PRIDE

Blaine was 21; this was his year. It was time for one of those $10 margaritas.

He caught the Muni train, standing next to a man in a shirt and tie.

"God, he must be at least 35," Blaine thought, "but he still works out. Big pecs."

"Going to Pride?" the man said, making eye contact, smiling through a gray mustache.

In a bright pink tank top and shorts, there was little doubt.

"Yep!"

"I gotta work. I'll miss it. I remember when I was a baby gay and Pride was like visiting the Emerald City."

Blaine giggled at his choice of words. The man stepped closer, looking down at Blaine, keeping that disarming non-threatening smile on his face.

"Wow, are we going to kiss? Is that okay?" thought Blaine nervously as they arrived at Civic Center.

The man leaned in and gently kissed Blaine on the ear, whispering, "Go get'em, Tiger."

QUIET

The commuter train car was full. The car's uncomfortable closeness, filled with people wearing earphones and staring down at bright devices, added to the weird silence.

Her phone rang, sounding louder than it was in the malaise of the commute. Her ringtone was Madonna's 'Like a Virgin,' much to the amusement of the fellow passengers.

The train pulled through a few more stations, the pillars of travelers bending slightly as the breaks were applied at each stop.

"Tampax wings, heavy flow. The green box," she suddenly blurted out into the headset.

It might as well have been announced through overhead speakers. Even people who had been lost in their devices turned to look at her.

"It's okay, dear," said an older woman, looking over her glasses, "I've been married for 40 years and my husband can't shop for me either."

After a momentary pause, the entire car burst out laughing.

AND THERE WON'T BE A SECOND DATE

He just kept talking.

"Last night, I meet this hot couple online. I show up with my trick bag and we had a great time," he continued.

It's not that I mind talking about sex or hearing about sex, but as a rule, it's not a first date conversation for me. But I already knew his favorite positions, and that he'd set up our date on his cell while getting dressed at this couple's house.

"And they have this adorable little dog, a cocklepoo or something, named Bowser. One of them is this real young Energizer bunny boy and the other, a muscle daddy type with hair everywhere."

"Let me stop you a second. They live in the Marina, in a yellow brick house?"

"Wow. Yeah. How'd you know?"

"You spent the night with my ex and his new boyfriend."

"Oh," he paused. Then laughing remorselessly, said, "Awkward!"

INTRODUCTIONS

He sat in the banquette nursing drip coffee, adding cream occasionally and humming Carly Simon as it hit the surface. Then, glancing over his screen, he noticed her.

She walked, no, she floated across the room. In a blue summer dress, old-fashioned pearls, and a white leather purse on her shoulder. He hated small-talk introductions. He'd formulate one in his head, then erased them with self doubt. He tried not to stare.

She ordered, in a surprisingly bass male voice, "Soft-boiled egg and toast. Thank you, darling."

Looking up again, suddenly, she was gone. He'd lost his opportunity. Then the waiter came by.

"This is for you," he said, placing a napkin on the table.

Written in perfect artful handwriting, "You're cute. Perhaps breakfast here together sometime? We're often here at the same time. When you smile, you light this whole dump up. I'm Margie. 415-555-5555."

PACIFIC

The cedar-plank siding had been bleached gray from summers in the fog and ocean mist. The deck gets a fresh coat of white every Memorial Day. The gaggle of friends with cocktails and fireworks of sudden laughter were a common sight.

At least one bewildered straight tourist walking the beach would ask us if we were all related because of our beards. The neighbor to the left, an accountant from Gilroy, just called us 'the beards.'

"Good morning, beards!" he would cheer, going by on a morning jog. Patrick was convinced that one day he'd start growing a beard and just join us.

I was up early, watching fog swirl through like we were at a mountain top. I stepped down onto the beach from the deck to feel the cool sand on my feet and let the cold fingers of the Pacific curl my toes.

ON OUR SLEEVES

By 1988, there had been 61,816 deaths in the U.S. alone. I was twenty-one.

Two years later, nearly twice as many Americans had died of AIDS as died in the Vietnam War. By the time I was thirty? 234,225 deaths. Forty? Nearly 600,000 deaths.

Just consider that for a second. Six-hundred thousand dead. That's the entire population of Denver or Portland or Seattle or Austin, dead. Twice the population of Minneapolis, three times the population of Madison, Wisconsin, six times the population of Salt Lake City or Boise, dead.

By the time I was twenty five, I'd attended more funerals than weddings. It was so important to remember everyone who lost. Nobody deserved to be a statistic. Nobody was going to be the emotional equivalent of an unmarked forgotten gravestone. Our community lived for remembering. To do otherwise was unthinkable.

We queers became the experts at grief. We wore it openly on our sleeves next to our battered hearts. Our personal calendars are always full of when friends and lovers lost the battle. Each of them live on through stories like this one. Stories about someone that touched our life in such a direct way, that you mark their passing each year on the calendar as a personal memorial day. When I was in my 20s, I had a couple that I called my 'gay' Mom and Dad. They define the early days of AIDS for me.

It was the summer of 1988 that I met Mark Spencer. Mark absolutely defined 'sparkle.' He was a cabaret singer and local variety show performer. He was always spit-shine polished, and everyone knew who was responsible.

Friends used to joke that his partner John was the stage manager for "The Mark Show." It was never meant with even a hint of disrespect. We were all jealous of the complete adoration that was apparent in both of them every time you were around them.

You'd see a slight ,gentle touch on Mark's collar while he was surrounded by boys telling some outrageously rude joke. You'd catch them stealing thick, bourbon-filled kisses in the kitchen at a dinner party full of house guests. Pictures of them with fabulously feathered '70s hairdos, powder blue tuxedos and thick rimmed glasses looking like extras from an extra campy *Magnum P.I.* episode, adorned the entry way to their home. They would tell beautifully detailed, different versions of the same story depending on who got started. Always on special occasions they'd tell of the night they came home together down the gravel driveway to their woodsy, small home. It was like listening to someone recite the most romantic of all fairy tales. Mark's little details always making John blush at the right moments. It all seemed perfect.

Watching him that day, he was the personification of celebration and remembrance. Even in Mark's death, John was the supportive partner, putting on the perfect send-off party, determined to get it absolutely right. It's crazy how I can remember that evening on the ocean vividly, right down to the most particular detail.

Mark's service was held at the labyrinth at Land's End. Out on the end of the world, with the setting sun bouncing off the water, lighting up the Golden Gate like a picture postcard. You had to walk down the earthen steps and find your way down to the sea. Once we'd all arrived, John went around the circle as people continued to greet one another. He handed each person a paper lantern. A deep reverent hush fell over all of us as we each realized Mark and John had made these in advance. Written on mine in John's perfect cursive handwriting was a long paragraph:

"We met you at the baths on a joyous Pride weekend. You had just turned 21. I am so excited to know you'll finish college and make a real difference in the world," I read, with tears welling up. "I know you'll be brilliant. You'll break through that trademark shyness of yours. I will miss you, bucky boy, but the world is going to get such a gift."

I looked up around the circle, witnessing how these personal messages were affecting everyone involved.

John walked out to the edge near the water and lit the candle in his lantern, passing it around the circle to the next person. The sun started below the horizon as everyone's lantern bounced with candlelight and started to fill with warm air, making them light in our hands. John let his go, and it seemed to hover, in fact, hesitate in his hands.

He spoke in this incredibly almost unbearable soft voice, "No. No. It's time for you to go, honeybear."

As if hearing his absolute command, the lantern lit off from his hands and floated up, catching the breeze, which took it up and out to sea, candlelight revealing that the entire surface of his lantern had writing upon it. He looked after it like a parent sending his child off to school on a fall morning. One by one, the lanterns in our hands followed suit, slowly rising into the sky and wandering away.

I'd always meant to keep in better touch with John. But Mark was right, I finished college, went to Africa in the Peace Corps, and my life had taken off like a rocket ship. I had always thought to myself that John had gone quietly and peacefully after his husband without regrets.

Twenty-one years later, there he was on Facebook. It was like a ghost came up on my computer screen. According to his profile, he'd gone on to get a doctorate and was now a counselor in Calgary. He was single, aggressively agnostic, and had a dog named Lucille.

He still had that calm smile, like the entire world had become a "Mark" for him to adore from across the room. The computer beeped, and a message from him came up: "I've missed you."

MEETING GEORGE

I was backpacking and staying in a small lakeside campground on Orcas Island. Moss hung from the trees, and my campfire seemed like it was the only one on the entire island. It was a rainy spring, and while that weather chases away most folks, it is precisely the kind of weather that calls my soul outdoors to watch the world refresh and start anew. It was all the more surprising when he walked out of the woods, soaking wet, to sit next to my campfire. He was a blonde lab with the most fascinating blue eyes. Almost intuitively, he joined me under my lean-to out of the rain, circling up next to me. We slept the night together, listening to the raindrops dance on the lake.

We sat the next morning over oatmeal and bagels, asking him what his story was. I reached out to pet him and he leaned in strong against my hand, communicating back how good it felt to be there with me. We walked into town and discovered that George had been left at a gas station, his owners getting on the ferry to the next island and never returning. He'd become a wandering mascot of sorts, with the local grocer setting out a bowl behind the store each morning and night like something out of *Lady and the Tramp*; doggy dinner for one.

There was never really a question about whether he wanted to come home with me. For the rest of my week on the island, we were inseparable. I explained to him that I had been left too, that she'd left me after 14 years together. My sense of solitude some of the time had chased her away. I told him we'd found each other on this island and perhaps we should hike together and become better friends. That night in the tent, he moved from the foot of the mattress and, despite his size, circled up against my chest. He returned with me to my small bachelor home on campus.

Back home, the sadness of the divorce returned. Despite having found a new home, there were reminders of the failed relationship everywhere in my life. George tolerated my morose dumpiness for a couple of days, but woke me up on the third day bouncing up and down on the bed early in the morning. He licked my hands and my neck and my ears. When I tried to hide under the blankets, he followed me there, finally finding my face. He licked 'til my beard was wet, finally collapsing next to me, pawing at my face playfully, but so very gently. It was the first time I saw that look in his eyes, "Come on; there is so much more to see." Over the next few months, he pulled me through the world, to farmers markets, through art festivals, making new friends at the dog park.

Each morning, I'd ring my meditation bell, put on soft music and meditate. He decided that next to me, head down in his paws was where he belonged during that spiritual time in the morning. He decided if it was important for me, it should be for him too. We'd breathe together and set our intentions for the day amongst the redwoods. This was the kind of moment that bonded us together so tightly. He understood my need for quiet and solitude, but became the exception to the rule. Even if we spent a quiet night in by the fireplace, he'd lay in a circle making sure I could feel him there. We'd make the walk to campus and he'd circle up on his bed at my desk. I have students that still write me asking about him, and always commenting on what an empathic dog he always seemed to be.

We'd spend Saturdays down at the coffeehouse sitting outside, sneaking him torn bagel pieces dipped in creamy coffee. He was never one of those to jump on people. He always approached, and particularly with small children, he learned this adorable little bow. You could feel the tension on the lead that he wanted to say hello. He'd approach and very slowly lower down to a sit. He'd then bow his head, welcoming them closer. He offered them peace and love like no other being I've witnessed.

He became such an integral part of my life that when he started slowing down I was in a bit of denial about it. The vet was compassionate with me explaining that George was sick, and wasn't going to get any better. She gently explained that we could take care of things at our home, and not have to make a big scene of it all at the office. The vet came by, we shared a cup of tea on the deck, and then she helped me give George the calmest send off possible.

On our first anniversary together, we had packed the car which always caused George to run around the house, wild with excitement. In the old pickup he'd ride along, his head on my leg, watching the trees go by through the window. We went up in the mountains. I knew a campground with a beautiful creek running through it, with a hike up through ancient trees. He would run ahead of me, always staying in sight, and turning his head back to me as if to say, "Come on, there is so much more to see." It was on our twelfth such anniversary, that I stepped out of the woods to the shore of the small pond. I set my pack down, reaching inside for the small wooden box. The not-quite-springtime mountain air swirled down around as I paused for a moment.

"You loved it here," I said as I opened the box, examining its contents. It was remarkable to me that a blue cloth collar, some off-white dust and a few small pieces were all that could be left. I ran my finger through the fine dust, then in a single motion, propelled it all over the surface of the quiet pond.

He had seen me through the largest changes in my life. He never gave up on me, despite times where I'd done so myself.

I smiled to myself, realizing that he was my most successful adult relationship.

THE KITCHEN

The dream broke suddenly and I was awake. I glanced over at the clock reading 4:30 a.m. I stumbled in the kitchen in my boxers and robe. The coffee maker sat in the same corner it had for 40 years, accompanied by a pair of fiesta ware blue coffee cups. Everywhere I looked, memories flashed and seared back at me.

I'd sat at that same old oak dinette admitting to my parents that I was gay, and that Harold was more than a roommate. She'd responded with cool hardness. I was simply never welcome there again. The worst of it was that Pop and I simply weren't allowed. I know that sounds terrible, but it was the truth.

This was the man who from the earliest age must have understood my view of the world, watching me fall in love with eighth-grade playmates, picking me up from theater rehearsals. I was always Daddy's good little boy. I'd gone off to school and made a good life for myself.

A few years back, my sister invited Harold and I to her wedding. Harold couldn't make eye contact with Mom, knowing how much pain her dismissal of us caused me and the rest of the family. Pop looked at me, across the room, trying his best. You could see her reach under the table and touch him when she'd catch him.

I've tried not caring. It doesn't work. I cared anyway. I tried for a while keeping the lines of communication open by sending notes and cards every holiday and birthday. None were ever responded to, and each day without a response is a new, raw wound. And I felt so utterly stupid and angry with myself after each unrequited outreach.

I'd truly given up hope, when one day I came home from a trip, and there was a phone message from the gallery.

"Some guy came in and bought one of your pieces. The big orange one, the streetlight? He wrote something really odd."

She handed me the check, and reading it, I began to tear up. Written in the memo on the check in my Dad's immediately recognizable handwriting was, "This is the best yet, boy."

Pop had figured out a way to contact me. He returned every six months to a year, always demanding to pay a little more than it was offered for, writing "Love this new direction you're on," "You keep getting better," and "Harold must be so proud of you" in the check memo.

We kept the checks in an envelope, treasured secret communiques received from behind enemy lines. My sister admitted that he'd bring the pieces to her, and they'd find somewhere to donate them, some way to send them to Dad's business contacts or my sister would put them up in her office.

She called one evening to let me know Mom had a stroke, and while they had her at the hospital, there wasn't hope that she'd recover. She died quickly and painlessly. Just as suddenly, there was the front pew in the church, with my sister, her husband, the twins, and next to Pop, me and Harold. The next few weeks were a blur of helping him get the house set up.

There I was, after all those years, right back in the kitchen at the crack of dawn.

"I betcha still eat bacon with that fancy-dancy, organicky, yoga-y diet of yers," Pop asked, working over the stove. "Coffee's on. I got some of that yellow poison you asked for. I figgered we'd go hikin'. Besides, why waste a beautiful day when it's given to you."

As I reached for the fridge to get cream, I noticed a photo on the door in a magnetic frame. It was a startlingly sexy, beautiful photo of her. She was in her 20s, laughing in the black and white light of a campfire.

"Yeah, I put away most of 'em, but that one stays," Pop said, noticing me stop.

"She's so happy, and beautiful..." I said, letting out a gasp.

"She really was, boy. She really was. But at some point she just forgot how to be happy, and I'm sorry for that, boy. I really am."

The next few years were an amazing renaissance for him. He embraced the widower patriarch role with gusto, doting on his grandkids and family, quietly rediscovering himself. He spent a lot of time traveling, sometimes taking Harold along as he got old. Harold and my Pop became best friends, and art critic buddies. He'd come and spend long weekends at our place out in the woods hiking, finding beach treasures to send to the grandkids.

Pop's been gone a while now. I guess it's part of the heartache of it all.

Pop had taught me that being awake at sunrise was a solitary gift to look forward to. I can remember sitting on the front lawn, he had his cup of coffee and cigar, me my cup of cocoa that was more marshmallows than cocoa. We'd sit there and watch everything reveal itself.

Particularly when fall comes around, I go out and walk in the darkness, the streetlights illuminating fall colors in the trees and swirls of fog. The harvest moon dancing with fading morning stars. I reach the coffee shop and I'm soon sitting in the park with the dog, as the first glimmer of dawn begins. It feels like this epic waterfall that's been filling all night long and when it finally starts to flow over the edge of the world, it grows faster and faster. Through the trees, the bright sun breaks the horizon.

I smile thinking of Pop, who in his quiet gravelly voice would say "Now boy, how could you want to miss this?"

ABOUT THE AUTHOR

As a self-described disciple of Henry David Thoreau, Robert B. McDiarmid is both a writer and activist. He works very hard to live an uncomplicated life in complicated times.

Robert resides in Palo Alto, CA with his husband David and their terrier companion, Miss Kate. An avid cyclist, he has participated several years in AIDS Lifecycle, a 550-mile bicycle ride from San Francisco to Los Angeles, and in the Friends for Life Bike Rally from Toronto to Montreal, Canada. In the spirit of giving back to the community, the entirety of his royalties are donated back to HIV/AIDS charities.

Robert is proud to be the author of *The House of Wolves* from Lethe Press, as well as a contributor to *A TASTE OF HONEY* from Dreamspinner Press, with his short story '*The Do-It-Yourself Guide to Getting Over Yourself.*"

He can be found at www.robertmcdiarmid.com, on Facebook at www.facebook.com/thoreauinsf and on Twitter @thoreauinsf.

He further authors a healthy cooking blog with recipes and instructional videos at http://www.bobscooking.com. Robert won a San Francisco Bay Area television cooking competition, *The Big Dish*, in December 2013.